LILY
OF THE
DESERT

SHARI L. TAPSCOTT

SILVER & ORCHIDS
BOOK FOUR

Also by Shari L. Tapscott

Crown and Crest

Knight from the Ashes

Forged in Cursed Flames

Fall of the Ember Throne

Rise of the Phoenix King

Royal Fae of Rose Briar Woods

The Masked Fae

The Gilded Fae

The Disgraced Fae

The Riven Kingdoms

Forest of Firelight

Sea of Starlight

Dawn of Darkness

Age of Auroras

Silver & Orchids

Moss Forest Orchid

Greybrow Serpent

Wildwood Larkwing

Lily of the Desert

Fire & Feathers: Novelette Prequel to Moss Forest Orchid

Eldentimber Series

Pippa of Lauramore

Anwen of Primewood

Seirsha of Errinton

Rosie of Triblue

Audette of Brookraven

Elodie of the Sea

Genevieve of Dragon Ridge

Grace of Vernow: An Eldentimber Novelette

Fairy Tale Kingdoms

The Marquise and Her Cat: A Puss in Boots Retelling

The Queen of Gold and Straw: A Rumpelstiltskin Retelling

The Sorceress in Training: A Retelling of The Sorcerer's Apprentice

Lily of the Desert

Silver and Orchids, Book 4

Copyright © 2017 by Shari L. Tapscott

ISBN: 9781978416543

Editing by Z.A. Sunday & A Fading Street Publishing Services

Cover Design by Trif Book Design

For Rahma:
Thank you for joining me on my written adventures!

I

BIRD'S EYE VIEW

There is something about harpies that I find incredibly disturbing. It's not the ink-black feathers that cover their tall, lithe, human-esque bodies, nor their birdlike feet complete with razor-sharp talons.

As I stare at the one in front of me, with her hauntingly beautiful face, obsidian eyes, tufts of feathers that protrude from her head in an owl-like fashion, and murderous sneer, I realize what it is.

I edge backward, bow drawn, with my eyes trained on her talons.

"Sebastian," I call as calmly as you please—as if we're sitting down for tea and not in an elaborate tree community high in the Eromooran forest. "How do you think she cares for all that hair? I mean, honestly, it looks better than mine."

"Lucia!" my scouting partner hollers at me from two

platforms down, sounding about five minutes past impatient. Probably because he's surrounded by two of the raven women himself.

The harpy lunges at me, talons glinting in the dappled sunlight that streams down from breaks in the canopy above. Moments before I lose an eye, I drop to my belly and roll to the side—somehow managing to keep my nocked arrow in place. Panting, I run for the rickety rope ladder that dangles not far away, thanking my lucky stars that harpies cannot fly—they can glide and do fluttery hops that remind me of baby birds trying new wings, but they can't just leap into the air and attack.

The harpy screeches from behind me, but I have no idea what she says because I do not speak *bird*.

"Just jump!" Sebastian yells as I secure my bow on my back.

Not happening. Sure, the next platform is only five feet down, but if I miss...

I glance at the shadowy, shrub-covered ground that's far, *far* below us. I gulp, and my leg starts to shake. The sharp rope digs into my hands, but I don't give in to my paranoia.

Unfortunately, my feathered friend has no qualms about leaping to the next platform, so as soon as I reach the bottom, she's already coming for me.

With no time to grab my bow, I pull my dagger from its sheath. It's a wicked weapon—dark, sleek, and deadly. But the harpy doesn't think twice about leaping forward, talons extended. Trapped between her and the edge, I meet her attack, knowing it's going to hurt.

LILY OF THE DESERT

I brace myself for her talons even as I slice her leg with my blade. She screeches again and catches me on the arm, just below my shoulder. The pain is incredible, and I hiss out a curse.

"Lucia!" Sebastian yells again as he climbs the ladder to reach my platform.

Filled with indignant rage and pain, I scream a battle cry, plow right into her midsection, and push her off the ledge. Before I tumble with her, I stumble back—only to have her grasp my wrist and yank me down. Just as my life flashes before my eyes, I'm pulled back. I collide with Sebastian's chest, and he wraps his arm around me to keep me from toppling over.

I extend my arms, hands out, steadying myself. Below us, the harpy makes a dreadful racket, though I don't know why she's so upset. It's not like she didn't coast down safely.

After I suck in several long, deep breaths, Sebastian unhands me. He lets me go, but it's not a gentle move.

"Are you insane?" he demands as he shoves a hand through his teak-colored hair. His green eyes flash with anger and residual worry, and if he hadn't just saved me, I might wonder if he was going to shove me from the platform himself.

Instead of answering him, I look down at my arm, which is inconveniently oozing blood. "Great," I mutter. "Now we're going to attract a whole murder of the beasts."

The nasty scavengers can smell carnage from a mile away.

Sebastian growls low in his throat and rips a ragged strip of fabric from his undershirt. Gentle as an ogre, he ties the fabric around my arm, making sure to really tighten it with the last knot.

"Um...*Ow*," I whine.

He flashes me a look and then steps back. "Other than that, are you all right?"

I scan my body for more injuries. "I think so. What did you do with your lovebirds?"

Sebastian wrinkles his nose. "I took care of them."

"You didn't kill them, did you?"

I don't have the stomach for that sort of thing. Killing a harpy is like killing a mermaid—they're just a little too human for my taste.

"Sleeping charm." He nods over the platform, and I look down. Sure enough, both the harpies are fast asleep, slumped next to each other.

"I see you've learned a few things from Adeline. Good thing you've spent so much time together."

He pretends to ignore the comment, but the tips of his ears turn red.

"You didn't lose the bracelet, did you?" he asks, changing the subject.

I slip my hand into the coin pouch at my side, checking to make sure it's still there. My fingers close around the delicate chain, and I shake my head.

Two days ago, the trio of harpies attacked Duke Rodge's carriage between Eromoore and Teirn. They stole everything of value, but the duchess only lamented the loss of her mother's pendant. Since we were conveniently passing through the province, we were hired to search for the harpies and bring it back.

I knew it would be an unpleasant job, but I've been willing to do just about anything to get my mind off a certain captain who sailed into the literal sunset three days ago.

Since the job paid well, and because he wasn't willing to let me run about forest-filled Eromoore alone, Sebastian came with me.

After I close the pouch, my hand absently runs over my dagger...my dagger with the tracking spell Avery will use to find us when he returns to Kalae.

The dagger that's *missing*.

"What's wrong?" Sebastian asks, noticing the look of horror on my face.

"It's gone!" Searching for it, I pat all over my body. I look at my scouting partner, aghast. "Sebastian!"

"We'll find it," he promises, and then he looks over the edge, probably suspecting, just as I am, that it went over with the harpy. He frowns at the ground. "That's inconvenient."

"What?" Cautiously, I make my way to the edge and peer down. Then I snarl, "I hate birds."

Far below, with a wicked look on her face that needs no translation, the harpy waves my dagger in the air for me to see. Then she flaps her nearly useless wings and takes off into the trees.

Livid, I turn to Sebastian. "We have to get it back."

Sebastian glances at the evening sky through the canopy above and rolls his neck in preparation for the inevitably long night ahead of us. "All right. Let's go."

2
MISSING DAGGER

"The heat will make you wish you were dead, but it's the spiders you have to watch for," Gorin says to Adeline just as Sebastian and I come stumbling into the tavern.

Not having seen us yet, the handsome, dark-haired Elrijan man continues, "The fist-sized tan ones—we call them sandskimmers—will make you ill, but it's the crimson assassins you must keep an eye on. There's no antivenom for their poison, but you won't die right away —no. It will kill you slowly, until finally, your heart simply gives out."

"What do they look like?" Adeline hesitantly asks, perhaps because she's morbidly curious, but more likely because we should know, considering we're going into their territory and all.

Before Gorin can answer, Adeline spots us. Or, more accurately, she spots Sebastian. The auburn-haired seamstress flies from her chair, nearly knocking it over in her haste to get to him.

"What *happened* to you?" Her hands flutter over Sebastian, looking for a spot to land and finding none because we are covered head to toe in forest grime, pine sap, and a few stray feathery wisps of harpy down.

"We found the harpies," I answer for Sebastian as I pull out a chair and collapse into it.

Flink, my wolfhound-sized lesser dragon quivers with excitement from underneath the table, and I pet the copper scales between his two tiny horns. After a few moments, he scratches an itch on his shoulder with his back foot and then lies down to continue his nap.

Adeline's about to press for details, but I don't want to speak of it. The sheath at my side is still empty, and I am sick. We never found the wretched harpy. With the aid of the spreading twilight, she was able to slip into thin air.

"Go on, Gorin. Tell us about your crimson assassins," I urge, crossing my arms over my chest in a closed-off sort of way.

Gorin eyes me, obviously wanting me to explain the sorry state of my appearance—but smart enough to avoid the subject. "They're good-sized compared to the little things you have around here." He presses the tips of his fingers to his thumb, making a circle with his hand. "About this big and hard to miss. Their bodies are blood red, with a black stripe running down their abdomen."

Adeline primly crosses her hands over her stomach, pretending she's not two seconds from passing clean out from the thought alone. She's about as squeamish as they come, but she's adamant about traveling with us into the desert to find a lily that grows only in Elrija.

According to Gorin, the legendary flowers, and the spring water they grow in, have astounding healing properties—to the point they'll reverse the aging process entirely. Gorin must retrieve one of the nearly mythical flowers so he may marry the woman he loves. Her father is ill, dying of a strange aging disease. The flower will cure him.

Since I owe Gorin a favor, we get to help him look for it.

Sebastian pulls out Adeline's chair, gallantly motioning for her to sit, and then he takes the empty seat at her side. When she turns her attention back to Gorin, Sebastian shoots her a wary glance. He hasn't come right out and said it, but I know he's not keen on the idea of her traveling with us. He's probably worried she'll be eaten. Honestly, I'm a little concerned about that too. From what Gorin has told us, his home kingdom isn't going to be a picnic.

"What about dragons? Or wyverns?" Unlike Adeline, I'm not squeamish, and I like to know what I'm in for. I lean forward, resting my arms on the table. "Oh—greater basilisks? I've heard they live in Elrija."

Gorin sweeps back his tousled black hair and flashes a friendly smile at the barmaid as she drops off our drinks before he answers. He takes a sip from his tankard and then taps the rim in thought. "We have dragons and a few species of wyverns, but they're far more timid than the ones native to your provinces. Greater basilisks live in caves to the northwest—I don't expect to head into their territory. After we pass the border, we go south to Stali for supplies, and then we'll head directly north."

We have just under three months to find the flower and return it to Kysen Okoro, or more specifically, until the first day of summer. The sands are already running through the proverbial hourglass. We officially left late winter behind and entered spring a week ago.

Coincidentally, Avery—the captain of the Greybrow Serpent, King Harold's favorite sort-of pirate, and the man who ruthlessly stole my heart—sailed on the day that marked the change of seasons. I was going to sail with him, but life doesn't always work out the way we think it will.

The captain promised he'll find me as soon as he's back on land, but I have no idea how he's going to accomplish that now. The ring he tossed me as the Greybrow Serpent sailed away rests on a chain at my neck, taunting me, making me homesick for a person instead of a place. Avery told me to keep it safe, said he has a question for me when he returns—and what girl wouldn't jump to conclusions when the man she loves yells *that* as he's sailing away?

"And...snakes?" I finally ask, though I'm not looking forward to Gorin's answer on this particular subject. I'm genuinely terrified of precisely two things: heights and all things that slither.

And the two together? You might as well carve my gravestone.

Gorin stares thoughtfully into his tankard. "Yes, we have a variety of serpents—all of them nasty. But my main concern is water. Every time I felt I was close to the map, I'd run out of reserves and have to turn back. The wells in Struin Aria are tainted."

Struin Aria is a city where the only alchemist known to study the lily's healing properties relocated hundreds of years ago, long before the city was mysteriously abandoned. According to rumor, he made the trek to the lily's spring every year, and he was the only man alive to know its location. Supposedly, he carried a map, and that map is somewhere lost in the fortress castle at Struin Aria.

Gorin's already been there and looked for it numerous times, but he decided it was time to involve professionals. Oddly enough, those professionals are us.

"Why didn't you take an alchemist with you?" Adeline asks, looking slightly less pale than she was a moment ago.

"An alchemist?" Gorin scrunches his brow, confused.

Adeline shrugs demurely. "It's nothing for them to clean the water. In fact, it's one of the first concoctions they learn when they go to the college in the guild."

I peer at her. She's always full of surprises. "How do you know that?"

"My father's the head of the mages' guild in Mesilca." She gives me a withering look when she sees my bafflement. "How do you not know that? Didn't you ever wonder how I learned so many spells?"

I purse my lips. Now that I think of it, she *does* seem to know an awful lot of magic for a professional dressmaker, but I thought that was just the way of it in Grenalda, the island territory where she's from.

Ignoring me, Adeline turns back to Gorin. "We can go to a local guild chapter and ask if they have any apprentices needing field work. If there are, the guild will send them with us free of charge."

"Really?" I ask.

Adeline nods. "They have to do a certain amount of time using their craft before the guild will certify them. When we return, we'll simply sign a few papers, vouching that their time was well spent."

"We'll have to find a guild first," I remind them.

We're in Eromoore, making our way to the Elrijan border. To say the province is provincial is giving it a lot of credit. It's the least inhabited area of all Kalae. Most of the land is forest. You can travel days without seeing a single soul.

It wasn't far from here that Sebastian and I became turned around in the woods and tracked down the greater fire hippogriff that started our illustrious scouting career. That's what got me in this mess with Gorin. In exchange for his ice charm, I was supposed to bring him back a phoenix feather. We never found the phoenix, but I didn't bring him back his ring either.

Gorin finishes his drink and slaps a few coins on the table, standing. Across the room, he calls to the barmaid, "Where's the nearest mages' guild?"

She glances over, smiling. "Thistlehorn, down the main road about twenty-five miles."

When he thanks her and turns back to us, the young

girl's smile dims with disappointment. Gorin's handsome, even if he's young. At nineteen, he's almost three years younger than Sebastian and me.

My business partner and I were born only a day apart in our little village, right in the middle of spring. It looks like we're going to spend our birthdays in the desert this year.

"We'll go first thing in the morning," Gorin says, excited to get back on the road.

"After we return the bracelet to the duchess," Sebastian reminds him.

Gorin's spark dims. "Yes, after that. But now we should get some sleep. It's late as it is, and we'll want to be up early."

If he could, he'd ride the entire way to the border without stopping. But it's understandable he's anxious to reunite with his betrothed. I've been separated from Avery for less than a week, and I feel like a caged panther.

And now I've lost the dagger.

Sharp panic strikes my core, stealing the breath from my lungs. The sensation is so acute, I can almost taste its metallic tang. How could I have been so foolish? How will the captain find me now?

Sebastian rises with the rest of us and scowls at the sorry state of his clothing. "I need to clean up. Lucia, you need to tend to your arm."

I glance at my makeshift bandage, nodding, and part ways with the others. As I walk to my room, despair threatens to choke me. Though it's nice having privacy, I wish I'd stayed with Adeline.

I turn my borrowed key in the lock and push the door open. A candle flickers on a table by the bed and a fire burns in the hearth—both try their best to make the small space cozy. The room is lovely, especially for one in such a small inn and tavern.

I set water to boil and prepare to clean the harpy's angry talon slash. I take my dear sweet time, stalling as long as I'm able because it's going to burn. When the kettle squeals, I know I can stall no longer. The wound stings like elemental ice, and I suck in a sharp hiss when I dab the cloth over it.

A soft knock sounds at the door. Letting the cloth fall back in the basin with a splash, I walk across the room to see who's in the hall.

Sebastian stands on the other side. Apparently he didn't mind cleaning up with cold water, because his hair is freshly washed, and he couldn't have taken the time to heat a kettle. Even though he'll be retiring shortly, he also changed his doublet and dirty trousers for a new, sharp set.

He doesn't say anything, but his eyes tell me everything he's thinking.

"I'm fine," I manage to say, even if my voice is listless.

He studies me for several more seconds, and the firelight dances in his green eyes. He's handsome, startlingly so. There was a time I was in love with him, but never like I love Avery.

Without a word, he steps in the room and jerks his chin toward a chair by the wash table.

"I've got it—"

"Sit down." His voice is soft—well, soft for Sebastian. "Let me help."

Because I'm afraid I'm going to break if I speak, I only nod and do as he says. With extreme care, he cleans the wound. "Where's your mother's astringent and salve?"

After you've known someone twenty-one years, you know certain things about them—like I never go anywhere without my mother's homemade concoctions. I used them on him once, almost a year ago in Mesilca. As if he remembers as well, he meets my eyes and gives me a tight smile.

The memory is bittersweet, but it doesn't conjure any long-forgotten feelings. Tonight, I'm simply glad for his company.

As always, the astringent stings with the fury of a thousand wasps, but the salve takes away the bite. Without feeling the need to fill the silence with conversation, he works quietly. It's comfortable between us again. I wasn't sure we'd ever reach this point, but I'm glad we have.

"There." He sits back on his heels and looks at me with such pity, I have to look away. "It's going to be all right—I swear it will."

"I lost it." I try to control my voice, but it wavers. "How..."

And though I try several times, I can't take in enough breath to finish. I end up doubled over, clutching my arms around my chest, trying to breathe.

"Come here." He laughs as he yanks me close, but it's a sympathetic sound. "Avery will find us." He pulls me back at arm's length, making me look at him. "He's the bane of my existence. You really think he'd disappear for good?"

I laugh through my tears, but the ache is still all-consuming. There's a knock at the door, and then it opens. Adeline's eyes widen with shock when she sees us, and then she notices my blotchy face. "What happened?"

In moments, she's kneeling beside us, her eyes filled with worry.

I turn to face her, knowing she'll understand far better than Sebastian ever could. "I lost the dagger."

"Oh, Lucia," she breathes.

Without further ado, she shoos Sebastian out of the room. Before he goes, he catches my eyes. "If you need anything…"

"Thank you."

Adeline pulls me to my feet. "Finish washing up. It will help—I promise."

In fifteen minutes, I'm as clean as I can be without a proper bath and in a nightgown that's as soft as a cloud.

Adeline sits on the bed, brushing my hair the way she says her sisters used to brush hers when she was young. "There is no one more resourceful than Captain Grey-brow—you know that. If anyone can track us, spell or no spell, it's him."

I nod, sniffling like a little girl. "You're right."

She's quiet for several minutes, and I stare into the fire, letting the dancing flames make me sleepy.

"I should hate Sebastian for the way he looks at you,"

Adeline says softly after several minutes of silence. "But it makes my heart melt when I see how sweet he can be."

I catch her wrist and look over my shoulder. "You know he doesn't love me—not like you love him. Not like I love Avery."

Frowning, she nods. "I suppose."

Adeline's quiet for far too long, and I turn. "What are you brooding about?"

"I just..." She trails off, perhaps rethinking her words. "I wonder if he'd like me better if I were like you. Adventurous, brave." She frowns, thinking. "*Brunette.*"

I laugh at the absurdness of that last part. Adeline's hair is gorgeous, and she knows it.

She smiles, but it's sad. "Part of me thinks that if he were inclined to fall in love with me, he would have done it by now."

"Or he simply hasn't admitted it yet." I cross my legs on the bed and face her. "You have to remember—he's Sebastian, and therefore the stubbornest man in all Kalae. Just because he hasn't *said* anything, doesn't mean he doesn't *feel* anything."

"Sometimes, I wish I were different—someone he would be more inclined to like."

Feeling unusually emotional due to the long day, I pull her into a hug. "Don't wish that, Addy. You're perfect just the way you are."

She sniffs, and I worry she's about to cry. "Thank you. But I'm still going to try to be braver—I'm going to help more." Looking determined, she nods, more to herself than me. "I mean it, Lucia. I'm going to be useful this time."

Though I'm not sure how she's going to accomplish that, I know it means a lot to her, so I nod. After a few more minutes, she retires to her own room. Exhausted and sore, I crawl under the covers and try not to think about the dagger that's missing from its usual spot under my pillow.

3

IN NEED OF AN ALCHEMIST

We reach Eromoore's mages' guild just after noon. We're in a quiet village, not much larger than our last, and the guild buildings are no bigger than taverns.

A gray jay chatters at us from the tree above as we walk up the guild's wooden steps. A few mages linger nearby—a man and woman flirting on the porch and an elderly gentleman reading a positively massive book in the sunshine.

Sebastian opens the door, and we filter inside.

Adeline's heels click on the wooden planks underfoot, and the noise echoes in the large room. A fire burns in a hearth in the middle of the floor, but the spring day is too warm for it, and it's quite hot inside.

Looking happy to have something to do, a woman hurries to greet us. "I'm Eliza. We are here to serve. How may our guild be of assistance to you?"

She looks so eager to please. I can't imagine she has much to do in this particular guild, out in the middle of nowhere.

Adeline steps forward. "We have a fieldwork request."

The woman nods like she knows exactly what Adeline's talking about. With a crisp, businesslike nod, she turns on her heel and motions for us to follow her. "This way, please. You will need to speak with the master." She glances back. "I'll see if I can squeeze you in for an appointment."

I dare a glance at Sebastian and flash him a smirk. His eyes sparkle at the absurdness of the statement, but he manages to hide his amusement.

Eliza gestures to a bench right by the fire. "Sit here, and I will see if Master Benjamin is available."

We look at it, uncertain. Sure, we could all fit on the bench—but only if we squeeze together. Unfortunately, it's the only bench in the "waiting" area, and Eliza's bound and determined to do this by the book.

She stares at us, waiting with a pleasant smile on her face.

Right.

Adeline sits first, positioning herself as close to the edge as possible. Sebastian follows. I sit next to Sebastian, and Gorin somehow squeezes in next to me.

Sebastian, having no room for his shoulders, awkwardly lays his arm on the back of the bench—but mostly across Adeline's shoulders. A nervous giggle escapes her before she can rein it in. Sebastian, looking extremely uncomfortable, stares at the fire.

"Don't pretend you aren't enjoying it," I whisper just loud enough only Sebastian will hear.

He shoots me a glare, but again, his ears turn pink. I like this new way of torturing my business partner. It's very satisfying.

"Comfortable?" Eliza asks brightly. "Would you care for refreshment before I speak with Master Benjamin?"

Feeling ornery, hoping to prolong Sebastian's embarrassment for as long as possible, I say, "I wouldn't mind—"

"We're fine," Sebastian interrupts. "Thank you."

As soon as Eliza disappears into the back, Gorin leaps to his feet, giving us more room. I join him, leaving Sebastian and Adeline plenty of space on the bench. She looks mildly disappointed.

In just a few moments, Eliza returns with a tall, white-haired man at her side.

"Lady Lucia," he says heartily. "Your reputation precedes you."

I never know how to answer things like that, so I simply smile.

"Eliza says you have a field position available?" he asks.

Adeline jumps in. "We're going on an expedition in Elrija, and clean water will be sparse. We require an alchemist who can travel with us, working along the way."

"Elrija?" Master Benjamin strokes his chin in thought. "You'll need someone brawny."

"We would prefer not to take someone with a delicate nature." I try not to glance at Adeline as I say it. Perhaps the statement would have been more accurate if I had said we didn't want to take *another* someone with a delicate nature.

After several moments of deep thought, the master nods. "I have just the man for you. He's not apprenticed long, but he's taken to it well, and he should have no trouble with simple water cleansing, if that's the extent of what you require."

We end up following the man down a flight of dark, narrow stairs and enter a huge, windowless room. Benches and tables are tucked everywhere there's a spare nook, and several people are hard at work. There are enchanters, bent over their workbenches, a man who appears to be crafting charms, and a small group of alchemists staring at a beaker of bubbling blue goo.

"Apprentice Edelmyer," Master Benjamin calls across the room.

Several people lift their heads, but only one man rises from his seat—a familiar man.

I'd almost forgotten how big he is, and in this crowd of lanky mages, the sight of him is almost comical. My mouth gapes open, and his nose flares with disgust. No matter his response to us, he stalks forward, not about to snub the head of the tiny guild he's somehow infiltrated.

"Yancey!" I say, half-irritated, half-relieved to see

that the previous duke of Mesilca's displaced son is alive and well. "Have you been here this entire time?"

Looking down as if I am a troublesome child, he narrows his eyes. "You didn't expect me to wait on that wretched ship forever, did you?"

"I was working on it," I mutter under my breath.

"Excellent!" Master Benjamin says, choosing to ignore Yancey's obvious distaste for our group. "You all know each other."

I sneak Yancey a wicked look, the kind that says I know he must play nice because the head of his guild is with us. He stares at me, his lips twitching in a mirthless smile—but only marginally.

"It just so happens that a fieldwork assignment has come up, Yancey, and I have recommended you for the position. I know you're fairly new to us, and it might seem I'm tossing you into it a bit early, but I have full confidence you're the right man for the job."

"You're sending me out," Yancey says, his voice terribly flat. "With *them?*"

Master Benjamin takes a step closer and lowers his voice as if he's about to share some great secret. "You're going to Elrija. Isn't that exciting? I almost wish I could go myself."

Yancey turns his eyes on me. "Elrija?"

"We're going to track down a lily that grows in a legendary spring that's said to contain water that reverses the natural aging process." I give him a one-shouldered shrug as if we do this sort of thing all the time, which honestly, it's starting to seem we do.

"Of course you are." He sighs deeply and nods at the master. "And what will I be doing while I accompany them on this merry mission?"

"You will be removing contaminants from various hydration sources."

It seems it's taking an awful lot of restraint for Yancey to keep a semi-pleasant expression on his face. "So simply put, I'm there to boil the water."

"Oh, come now, Yancey," I say cheerfully. "You know there's more to it than that. You might have to strain it first."

Before Yancey can respond, Master Benjamin steps in. "With the amount of studying you've done in this last month, and this field assignment behind you, when you return, I see no reason why I cannot elevate your status to journeyman—as long as you pass the testing, of course."

Oh, and Yancey wants that. I can see it in his eyes. But is he willing to accompany us into the middle of the hot, *deserty* nowhere just to skip another five months' worth of studies?

"All right," he finally says, but he's not happy about it.

Unable to help myself, I wrap an arm around his back —more like his waist because he's so tall. "Oh, Yancey! Just think of the fun we'll have."

"Just think."

Then, so only he will hear me, I whisper, "How badly do you want to knock me to the ground with your fun little wind charm?"

He gives me a bare smile. "So badly."

"Then it's all settled," Master Benjamin says, not having heard our exchange. He claps his hands together, seemingly delighted. "Go see Master Len, and he will set you up with your supplies."

Yancey nods, and without another word, he walks away.

4
WELCOME TO ELRIJA

To reach Elrija, we must travel west. We continue through Eromoore and skirt through the lower tail of Bellaray. The trip only takes about a week, but Gorin is eager to arrive.

The elevation drop from the mountainous province to the Elrijan border is staggering. We make one last descent from Bellaray. In front of us, the tan desert spreads as far as the eye can see. Our road takes us into the foothills, past tall sandstone bluffs and red slickrock, through rolling hills covered in dry, brown grass and intermittent prickly, gray-green brush. Over it all, stretches an impossibly blue sky. The contrast is almost painful.

We've met several caravans, one entering Kalae and the other heading into the heart of the dry lands.

Our carriage bumps along at a sedate pace, and I'm antsy to move. I stick my head out the window for the dozenth time. Not far off, where the road goes through two layered cliffs, sits the border village of Bale Traore. Everyone who wishes to enter Elrija must go through one of the border communities—whether they like it or not.

And Yancey doesn't like it.

As I stare out the window, looking at the land that is so different from anything I've ever known, Gorin and Yancey argue over what ingredients the apprentice alchemist will have to relinquish at the border. Apparently anything and everything may pass into Kalae, but the Elrijans are a little more particular about what they'll allow in their kingdom.

"They'll confiscate live plants," Gorin says calmly, especially considering they've been over this before. "And you can buy all of it dried once we reach Stali."

Yancey huffs out a frustrated breath. "But I've told you—dried isn't as potent."

"I understand that—I do. But, honestly, you'll be hard-pressed keeping your herbs and whatnot alive in Elrija. Spring is not pleasant as it is in Kalae—it can be scorching, and the air is dry. I'm afraid your plants will die, even if you manage to sneak them in. And if they catch you with them, we'll be held up for at least a week. Worse—you might be blacklisted from the kingdom."

The two continue to argue. Adeline fell asleep about a half hour ago, and her head rests on Sebastian's shoulder. I'm not sure how it got there, but Sebastian doesn't seem to mind. She'll have heart failure when she wakes up.

I yawn and wish that I'd taken a nap myself. Who

knows how long we'll have to wait for the carriage that goes between the border village and Stali, the large city where we'll buy our supplies and start our expedition.

Less than half an hour later, we roll into Bale Traore. I'm the first out of the carriage, and I hurry to the luggage rack to make sure Flink didn't bump right off the back as we went down the winding, rocky road.

But my fears are for naught. The dragon is fast asleep, flopped on his back, belly to the sun, front leg twitching as he dreams.

Sebastian and Gorin make their way to the border guards who lounge next to the sturdy wooden gate. As soon as Flink is down, the driver begins with our luggage. The first trunk hits the ground with a thud, and a cloud of dust rises into the air.

"Ech," Adeline says, eying the dust and fanning herself with her hand. "It's already hot."

I glance at the sandstone mountain range in the distance. "The heat's only going to get worse."

She turns her attention on Sebastian and watches him with a wistful look. "Don't I know it."

Our sun-worn driver glances at her with appreciation, and she narrows her eyes, giving him a silent look that clearly says, "Not even in your wildest dreams."

She takes me by the arm and pulls me away from the carriage. I laugh as we meander through the sandy courtyard. Bale Traore is tiny but enchanting. The architecture is entirely foreign—made of clay and stone with intricately carved details. There's a fountain in the middle of the square, and water cascades from the tall statue at the center. The breeze catches the mist and blows it in our direction. I close my eyes, relishing the temporary respite from the heat.

Gorin wasn't lying. This isn't temperate spring weather. It's *hot*.

A few children chase each other around the fountain, and several women chat under awnings. They wear long, colorful skirts and sleeveless bodices in jewel colors. The Elrijan style is not that dissimilar to ours in Kalae, but their colors are bolder, and their jewelry is heavier and far more showy. In the sun, they wear lightweight hooded shawls and scarves to protect their skin from the harsh light.

"Yancey doesn't look pleased," Adeline whispers.

I follow her eyes to where the men stand with the border guards. Gorin and Sebastian stand, arms crossed, watching the exchange between Yancey and the men. He towers over them, intimidating as they come, but the guards do not flinch.

"Apparently they won't let him bring his plants," I whisper to Adeline, trying not to laugh.

We end up finding a spot on the ledge of the fountain while we wait. Flink watches the children, intrigued with their squeals, and finally falls asleep at our feet. The men argue for over an hour, but an agreement is reached. Now it's apparently Gorin's turn to be upset.

"What now?" Adeline asks as we watch Yancey stomp away.

I shake my head and stand. "I'll see what's going on."

"We don't have a week!" Gorin growls, tossing his hands up in the air.

The guard nearest him tenses. "There is nothing we can do about it. The coach will get here when the coach gets here."

The man's armor is leather and sleeveless, and it puts his massive muscles on display. I'm not sure Gorin, who's strong but in a young, lanky way, wants to pick a fight with this man.

Sebastian sets an arm on Gorin's shoulder, likely thinking the same thing as I am. "Gorin—"

Agitated, Gorin shoves a hand through his dark hair and strides across the courtyard. When he's out of earshot, he closes his eyes and growls, trying to hold in his anger. He sees me when he opens his eyes, and his shoulders sag with defeat. "We don't have a week to spare, Lucia."

He sounds so dejected, my heart hurts for him. And for all I know, he's right. I don't have the slightest idea how long it will take to find the lily.

But a tiny part of me, perhaps a prideful part, says, *how hard can it be?* We found the Moss Forest orchids; we did the impossible and returned from the forbidden waters with a sea fire ruby.

This lily is going to be a walk in the garden. After all, there's a map leading right to it. Of course, we must find the map first—but after that, it will be smooth sailing.

Sailing.

And once again, I'm reminded of Avery. It feels as if a

lead weight has been placed on my chest, and it takes me several long moments to catch my breath.

The captain's doing his job, and I'm doing mine. And the sooner I finish here, the sooner I can put my mind and efforts into finding him.

"Let me talk to them," I tell Gorin. "I'll see if I can work something out."

"You think you can make something appear out of thin air?" he asks. There's no real bite in his tone—just exasperation.

I raise an eyebrow. "Gorin, I'm in this mess because I know how to get what I want."

We both know that if I hadn't sweet-talked him that night two years ago for information on the location of a phoenix, he wouldn't have given me his great, great grandmother's charmed ice ring, and I wouldn't owe him a favor.

A real smile plays at his lips. He jerks his head toward the guards. "Talk to them then."

Tucking a wayward strand of hair behind my ear, I adjust my corset belt and fix a pleasant expression on my face. Then I lock eyes with the guard who dismissed Gorin and make my way toward him.

He nudges his friend, and the other man turns to me as well. From the corner of my eye, I can see Sebastian loosen his stance and step back, looking away as he tries not to laugh.

"My lady." The guard bows his head. "How may we be of assistance?"

I look down, fluttering my eyelashes like I've seen Adeline do so many times. "You already know."

"Like I told your friend, there's nothing—"

"What's your name?" I ask, stepping a smidgen closer.

The guard gulps. "Aaron."

"Aaron, you look like a capable sort of man. Tell me, what would you do if you needed to get to Stali as soon as possible?"

"I'd ride there, my lady."

"And do you perhaps know of someone we can buy horses from?"

He thinks about it for a minute, and then he winces. "Yes, but you don't want—"

"I do want." I nod. "I really do."

Aaron glances at the other guard, and I take a moment to turn to Sebastian. "Do we have it in the budget to buy a few horses?"

And though he looks like he wants to roll his eyes, he says, "If we can strike a good deal."

I turn back to the guard. "There you have it. Take us to someone who will make us a deal."

The guard shakes his head, but his eyes crinkle at the corners as he gives in. "All right."

"Excellent!"

Sebastian follows me when I turn away. "Honestly, Lucia. What would Avery say if he knew you were flirting with the border guards?"

I shoot him an incredulous look. "Please. He would tell me job well done."

"He probably would." Sebastian sounds disgusted, but there's good humor behind it. "But a horse? You don't ride."

"I'll figure it out, won't I?"

Before we're back to the group, I shoot Gorin a victorious smile. In turn, he gives Yancey a friendly shove, for which the big brute only scowls.

"I wonder if Adeline can ride?" Sebastian muses out loud.

Turning my head, I widen my eyes and press my hand to my chest. Purposely breathy, I say, "Perhaps you'll have to ride *together*."

"You know, sometimes you're intolerable."

"And sometimes you're a snob."

"Shameless flirt."

"Incurably arrogant."

We share a smile and join the others.

"We're purchasing horses," I announce proudly.

Gorin looks surprised. "Horses? Are you sure?"

I'm momentarily startled by his shock. "Yes...why?"

"It's just that horses aren't the standard form of equine transportation here in the desert."

"If not horses, what?"

Yancey, who's sulking next to Adeline scowls and nods behind me. "Look for yourself."

And there Aaron is, leading our new form of transportation to us.

"But..." I say, losing my train of thought as the sorry creatures plod toward us. "Those are..."

Aaron grins. "The finest mules in Elrija."

5

FOUR MULES AND A DONKEY

"I'm sorry," I say to Aaron, setting my hand on my hip. "I didn't order mules."

"To be fair," the guard says, smiling in a rather devilish way, "This little lady is a donkey. The rest are mules."

And those mules must be crossed with draft horses because they are massive creatures.

"We figured your friend here needed something a bit larger." He nods toward Yancey, who in response looks like he's going to punch him. I sidle in front of the alchemist, just in case.

The little jenny stares at me with her dark brown eyes, and her long ears twitch. I have no idea why, but I get the distinct feeling she's sizing me up.

"Do you want them or not?" Aaron asks.

"No," I begin to say, but Sebastian cuts me off.

"Yes. They will suit us fine."

Feeling a touch like Yancey, I scowl at the mules as

Sebastian haggles with the guard. The beasts are apparently worth their weight in gold in Elrija. Finally, Sebastian talks them down to a reasonable price.

Flink tugs on his lead, sticking his snout in the air to investigate the newest members of our expedition. Adeline walks him over, and the donkey leans down to greet him. Horses are usually hesitant of Flink, but the jenny is either too stupid to fear him or smart enough to know he's harmless. I have a feeling it's the second one.

"What are we going to do with our trunks?" Adeline asks.

Gorin strokes the mule closest to him. "The animals are large. Yancey, of course, will have to ride on one alone —" He steps away from the alchemist and grins. "But two of us can double on another, which will leave one for our gear. It's only a few hours to Stali."

"Adeline's slight. She should ride with Sebastian," I volunteer.

The pair stares at me, both with differing expressions. Sebastian looks at me like I'm a meddling aunt, but Adeline looks like she's going to faint.

"Yes, that will work," Gorin says, not even realizing the turmoil my suggestion has caused. "They've given us the all clear to pass through—" Gorin stops when Yancey says a very naughty word.

Apparently the alchemist is still pouting over his loss of plants.

"Let it *go*," I say under my breath.

Our ever-happy guide shoots Yancey a wry look and finishes, "So let's get on with it."

6

DRAGON ON A MISSION

The valley we travel is gold and rust, and the evening shadows sharpen the mountains and hills. It's early still—there will be another few hours of light—but animals are already out. Tiny spotted kalli deer roam in small herds, eating the twiggy sage-colored ballo brush. The plants have a sharp, earthy smell to them, not exactly pleasant. It doesn't stop the deer from snacking on them.

Red sandstone mountains rise in the distance, but we're smack dab in the middle of the foothills. There's more vegetation than you would guess from looking at the valley from afar. Along with the dry, brown grass and ballo brush, there are several different types of prickly-looking weeds and short plants with a multitude of tiny leaves. Some are even covered in purple buds, and I imagine it will be quite a display when they bloom.

Stali grows in front of us. It's far larger than tiny Bale Traore. The buildings are made from the same light tan clay of the desert, and apparently, the blacksmiths here are artists. The side of one of the buildings closest to the road is overlain with a sheet of black iron with a repetitive pattern of decorative cut-outs. Lanterns hang in the streets, just like in the cities of Kalae, but there's nowhere like this in the provinces.

The city is built right on top of the rolling hills, so the houses, shoppes, and the tremendous towering fortress are all on different levels, making Stali seem very tall. Restaurants have opened their wrought iron gates to the public, and patrons sit on terraced patios, sipping tiny cups of what smells to be the most fabulous coffee ever created and eating foods that have my mouth salivating.

I'm mesmerized, thoroughly enchanted by the newness of it all. And then I remember my dragon.

We let him roam freely while we traveled. He likes it here. It's warm and dry, and he happily wandered about, staying with us for the most part. But here...

Well, there's food.

Before the dragon can cause havoc in yet another kingdom, I pull my donkey to a stop and call out to Gorin, who's just ahead of us. "Have you seen Flink?"

Gorin looks around and frowns. "I haven't."

I turn back to Sebastian and Adeline, who are looking quite cozy on their shared mule. "Do you know where Flink went to?"

Before they can answer, I spot the dragon far down the street, making his way toward a meat stand. People stop to gawk at him, but he is a dragon on a mission, and he pays them no mind.

37

I give my donkey a good nudge, trying to get her to move faster. Unfortunately, she seems to have one speed only—slow. Giving up, I leap from her back. Unaccustomed to riding, my muscles nearly give out. I stumble forward, yelling Flink's name.

Behind me, Sebastian hollers at me, but I'm already running through the street, dodging carts, people, and traps.

I holler again, and this time I know the rotten dragon hears me. To my great astonishment, Flink stops and looks over his shoulder, meeting my eyes. He stares at me for three whole seconds.

And then he makes a run for it.

People look at me like I'm a mad woman as I go racing after him, yelling like a banshee. The demon dragon is faster than he looks. I trip over a loose cobblestone, almost falling on my nose. I'm so mad, the awful beast better hope I don't catch him.

He runs right past the meat stand, turns a corner, and goes down several more streets. People yell as he races past, but no one is brave enough to grab him.

Finally, he takes a left when he should have gone right, and he ends up in an alley with a dead end. I stumble to a stop, doubling over as I try to catch my breath.

"F...Flink." I gasp for air. "Come *here.*"

His amber eyes dart this way and that, looking for another escape, and he lowers his head in shame.

"No," I croak. "I will not feel sorry for you."

Flink drops to his belly and flattens his flightless

wings against his body, trying to make himself as small as possible.

Once I'm quite sure I'm not going to keel over, I stalk over to him and clip the lead to his harness. He makes a churring noise and rubs his head against my side, sweet as can be.

I glare at him and walk him back to the main street. The only problem is, I have no idea where we're at.

"Fabulous," I say as I look around, trying to find something that's vaguely familiar.

The two of us gawk at the city as we attempt to find our way back to our group. We've entered a market district, and there are stands everywhere. Colorful striped awnings cover the peddlers, and they call out to me as we pass. One man sells spices, another bolts of delicate fabric. There's a woman with exotic, hothouse flowers, and another stand specializes in antiques.

But what catches my attention is the man selling enchanted weapons, right here, out in the open. I stop in front of his stand, my mouth embarrassingly agape.

The man across from me smiles in a knowing way. "First time in Elrija?"

"Um..." Beautifully crafted, *new* arrows glow blue, taunting me. I look up at him. "Yes?"

It's one thing to find ancient enchanted weapons— Avery has a whole slew of them. But it's an entirely different matter to find new ones.

"Enchantments are illegal in Kalae, but not in Elrija," the man explains.

I stare at the arrows for a long time. If I don't buy

them, I'll surely need them. But are they necessary? I've never needed that sort of weapon for anything but a siren, and we won't encounter anything like that out here in the desert. It's not like this is going to be a difficult mission. We'll run into a few scorpions, a snake if I'm extremely unlucky.

And the arrows are expensive.

After several moments of indecision, I thank the man for his time and reluctantly walk away.

I scan the square, trying to get my bearings. People mill about everywhere—most are of Elrijan descent, with dark hair, warm skin, and deep chocolate eyes, but there are quite a few people who look like they're from the provinces too. There's a woman in fitted trousers and a long tunic, with a mess of blond curls tied up in a knot on her head. She haggles with a woman in a stall, and from their bright eyes and sharp words, I can tell they barter often.

A couple sits on a patio across the street, heads bent together, deep in conversation. She's Elrijan, but his hair is bronze. His skin is very tan though, which makes me think he's been in the desert kingdom for months if not years.

Flink and I step aside as a caravan passes through. They are heading east, likely back to Bale Traore and the provinces. People cast my dragon curious glances, enchanted with him. The attention makes him puff up like a peacock, and he struts with his head held high.

We end up following the caravan into a large square. On the way, we pass a man hawking sandals, a woman who insists I need a beaded shawl, and a little boy trying to sell me a "genuine" charisma charm. The square is even busier than the streets.

Not that being in a new place makes me nervous, but the sun is beginning to creep lower in the sky.

As I debate which way we should go, Flink sits on his haunches and sticks his snout in the air, taking in all the smells the new city has to offer. I look around, hoping to find some clue as to where we ended up.

"Have you found yourself lost, lovely Lady Adventuress?" a man says from behind me.

Instantly on guard, I turn. Even though I'm a medium height, the owner of the voice towers over me. He wears a drab brown vest and trousers just a shade lighter, and though he knows who I am, his dark eyes and warm complexion lead me to believe he's Elrijan. His features are too sharp to be considered handsome, but there's something compelling about him nonetheless.

"Are we acquainted?" I ask, though I'm sure I've never met this man.

"No, my lady. I'm afraid your infamy has followed you all the way to Stali."

That little statement makes me uneasy, but we're not *that* far from the provinces, not yet at least. I suppose it makes sense that there are those here, especially near Kalae's border, who will know who I am.

"I'm afraid I'm at a disadvantage," I say, still leery of the man since he came out of nowhere. "You know who I am, but I don't know you."

He smiles, and though the expression appears

genuine, there's just something about him that sets me on edge. For one, it's impossible to tell how old he is. At first, I'd pegged him to be far older than I am, perhaps twenty-eight or twenty-nine, but now I'm not sure. He might be older than I estimated—or he might be younger. It's disconcerting.

"My name is Akello, and I am at your service." He bows like a man accustomed to our Kalaen ways, with one hand on his back and the other stiff at his waist.

I study him for another moment and tighten my grip on Flink's lead. "Are you in the provinces often, Akello?"

He gives me a cryptic shrug that does nothing to ease the slimy feeling of dread making its way through my veins.

"Please do not think me presumptuous, but may I escort you to dinner, Lady Lucia? If I am not mistaken, this is your first time in Stali, and the city has much to offer."

I begin to shake my head, but the man is already hailing a carriage. The driver cannot be older than my youngest sister, Kirsten, who is only eight. No matter, the boy steers his single donkey toward us. The small wagon is just large enough for two, more a trap than a carriage.

"I'm sorry. I must find my companions." I'm already hedging backward.

Isn't this a lovely position I've found myself in? I cannot hurry away when I do not know the right route— who knows where I'd find myself? And I believe it's smarter to stay here in this busy square than end up in a deserted district when night falls.

Akello fixes his eyes on me and gives me a wry smile. "I've come on too strong, haven't I? You're looking to make a hasty getaway."

The boy in the trap looks between the two of us, fidgeting with the reins.

The humor in the man's eyes eases my worry, even if only slightly, and I roll my shoulders. "Perhaps a little."

He ducks his head in amusement.

"Forgive me," he says, and then he looks up, pinning me with his gaze. "I admit I was surprised to find you here, my lady, and I'm afraid my zealousness got the best of me."

Though I never know how to answer when people say things like that, I offer him a small smile.

Akello waves the trap away. With a frown, the boy clucks at his donkey.

"Wait." Akello flicks the boy a gold coin. "For your trouble."

The young driver's eyes light, and he leaves with a grin on his face.

After speaking with him, I don't feel as uncomfortable as I did a few moments ago, and I'm just debating asking him if he could help me find the others, when I hear my name called from across the square.

And there Sebastian stands, looking put out as he scans the crowd. A smile tugs at my lips, and I'm struck with intense affection. We've been through a lot in the last few years, but somehow, we've come out of it unscathed. He's still here for me, and he always will be. Just like I'll always be there for him.

SHARI L. TAPSCOTT

Akello follows my eyes across the square, and he frowns. "Friend of yours?"

I stand on my tiptoes and give Sebastian an exaggerated wave. "From the time we were little."

"Your business partner, I assume?"

I give him a sideways glance. "That's right."

"I figured, seeing as how your captain is at sea."

This time, I narrow my eyes. "You certainly know a lot about us."

The man steps a smidgen closer and leans down suggestively. "What can I say? I'm a fan of your work."

Sebastian finds me, and his gaze automatically falls on Akello. His expression hardens, and he strides to us, narrowly avoiding the traffic in the busy street.

Narrowing my eyes at the man across from me, I step back. "Captain Avery, and I, we're..."

Well, that's difficult to explain. But we are certainly *something*.

"Engaged?" Akello asks, but from the humor in his eyes, I can tell he knows the answer.

"Well, not exactly, but—"

"Is he courting you?"

"I'm not sure you could say that precisely—"

A slow smirk builds on Akello's face, one that makes me more than a little uncomfortable. "And he did leave you when he went back to sea, did he not?"

I square my shoulders to him. "Yes, but it's—"

"Complicated?"

Growing quite agitated, but wanting anything but, I take in a long, deep breath. "I suppose you could say that. But Avery will meet me as soon as he's back to the mainland."

Sebastian's halfway to us, and he stops to let an elderly woman pass in front of him. I wish he'd hurry up.

Akello takes another step in. "Indulge me, if you will. What's the sign of a good captain?"

I cross my arms and wait for him to continue.

"You don't know? Well, I will tell you: they value their ship and crew above all else. So, tell me, what does your Avery love more. You? Or the sea?"

A lump forms in my throat, and I try to swallow.

He lowers his voice to a whisper. "There's not a lot of water in Elrija, my lady. What makes you so certain he's coming for you?"

Before I lost the dagger, I was confident. But now?

"Because he swore he would," I say with a lot more confidence than I feel.

Akello laughs under his breath and steps back, creating much needed distance between us. "The word of a pirate."

I bite my tongue and glare at him.

"Pleasure meeting you, Lady Adventuress. I do hope our paths cross again." He gives me a friendly look that feels anything but and walks away, nodding at Sebastian before he slips into the crowd.

"Who was that?" Sebastian asks as soon as he reaches me, gesturing toward the street.

That vague feeling of unease returns. "One of my admirers."

Sebastian rolls his eyes. "I thought we left that in Kalae."

"So did I."

"We need to find the others before they get too far ahead."

I tug on Flink's lead and follow Sebastian, but I glance over my shoulder as I leave the square. There is no sign of the man.

7

SOMETHING FOOLISH

B uilt on a hill, the Stali Caravanserai is the highest building in the city beside the fortress castle. It's lovely with lush gardens of pink Elrijan hibiscus and graceful, statuesque palm trees. A shallow, rectangular pool of water takes up most of the courtyard, with a wooden footbridge spanning it. There's koi in the pond, and tiny, golden frogs rest on thick lily pads.

It's nearing twilight, and men in crisp linen trousers and jackets light the iron hanging lanterns.

With its white stone construction and artisan-crafted iron balconies, it's by far the loveliest inn I've ever stayed in. Scattered around the pool, half a dozen caravans have stopped for the night. They have their wares available to the public, and people meander through, looking at the goods and enjoying the beautiful evening.

The hot day has cooled to the perfect temperature, and the smell of blooming jasmine is in the air.

Avery would love it.

I rub my chest, willing the fresh bout of worry to go away. I feel every single mile I put between us, every hour, every minute.

Gorin discusses something with our group, and though I'm standing with them, my mind is too busy to pay attention. We stand at the entrance of the caravanserai, and a boy has already collected the mules and my donkey. He promised our luggage would be taken to the lobby and would be waiting for us at the front desk.

Elrija certainly knows how to do posh.

"Three days at the most," I vaguely hear Gorin say.

Sebastian shakes Gorin's hand. "Safe travels."

Finally, that catches my attention. I turn to our guide. "Wait. Where are you going?"

"To Kysen Okoro," he says slowly, likely because he already explained all this once. "I'll be back by sundown tomorrow."

"Kysen Okoro?" I ask. "Isn't that the king's city?"

A strange expression crosses Gorin's face, but only for a moment. "That's right."

Before I can ask him what business he has there, Yancey says, "Is it the location of Elrija's main guilds?"

"All except the fishermen's association. It's located in Tilbarro, near the Dranyan Sea."

"Let me come with you." Judging from Yancey's tone, it's not a request. "Thanks to your border guards, I'm short on basic supplies."

Gorin thinks about it for a moment. Though he wants to object, he finally agrees.

We say our goodbyes, and Gorin and Yancey head toward the stables to collect their mules before their things are taken inside.

Sebastian, Adeline, and I stand together, looking at our surroundings. For the first time in a long while, we have nothing to do.

"There are worse places to take a short holiday," Sebastian says after a few moments.

He's not the only one who thinks so. We're surrounded by couples. Couples strolling hand in hand. Couples tossing coppers into the koi pond. Couples sharing sweet kisses when they think no one is looking.

There are young couples, old couples, and couples of all ages in between. It's nauseating.

Adeline catches my eye and shares my look of frustration. There will be none of that for us.

Well, there could be for her, but she'll have to make the first move on Sebastian.

Looking at the situation objectively, as I am able to now, I see why I never knew how Sebastian felt. Because he is like stone—idle. If Adeline doesn't corner him, they'll stay in their current friendship forever.

If I had been more forward, if I'd been braver, we would probably be together now.

Thank goodness I wasn't brave.

"I'm tired." I tap Flink to get his attention and start inside. "Let's secure our rooms."

The lobby is horribly ostentatious, but it is pretty. The floors are shining white marble, and at the center is a decorative tile mosaic done in vibrant, rich shades. Floor-to-ceiling windows surround the room, draped in blood red velvets. At the back is a polished black granite counter, and several attendants wait to assist guests with their various needs.

"Welcome," a woman with a warm, easy smile says. Like the men outside, she wears an outfit of cream linen. "How may I be of assistance?"

Stepping up to the counter, Sebastian says, "We would like three rooms."

The woman nods and opens her ledger. "Names please."

Sebastian tells her, and her eyes flicker with recognition when he gets to mine. Surely I don't have another fan.

"Would that be Lady Lucia Linnon of Reginae?" She leans over the counter and smiles at Flink as she adds, "Lovely dragon."

"Um...thank you. And yes, I'm Lucia Linnon."

Without explaining her strange reaction, she scratches something into her ledger and hands us three keys. "Enjoy your stay. If you require anything, please inform any of our staff, and we will do our best to accommodate you."

Shaking off her odd reaction, exhausted and sore from the ride, I take my key. "Do you have a bathhouse on the premises?"

"The finest in all Elrija."

"Perfect."

"I'll have your things brought up right away," she

assures us, and then she smiles at the patron waiting behind us.

I turn to Adeline and Sebastian. "I'm tired. I'm going to drop Flink off at my room, visit the bathhouse, and then go to bed."

"You should eat," Sebastian says.

I wave his concern away. "I'll scrounge up something."

Adeline demurely coils a loose strand around her finger, not quite looking at Sebastian. "I was hoping to try that restaurant we passed—the one with the outdoor terrace. It smelled just lovely."

And looked insanely romantic.

Sebastian, clueless as always, nods absently. "That sounds fine. Come with us, Lucia. Don't be a killjoy."

Silently, Adeline begs me to decline.

"You two go on." Before Sebastian can argue further, I give them a quick wave and head to the winding staircase at the back of the building. "I'll see you in the morning."

The truth is, even if I didn't feel for Adeline's plight, I have no desire to eat, and I'd be terrible company. All I want to do is wash the donkey hair and desert off me, lie on my bed, and obsess over the dagger I lost.

With its romantic, exotic atmosphere, I cannot imagine a more depressing place to stay, but it's the only respectable inn in Stali. Not so long ago, I worked as a barmaid at whatever establishment would take me. I suppose I've become spoiled in the last year.

With a sigh, I push my door open and peer inside,

dumbfounded.

"Fancy, Flink," I murmur. "Looks like we're moving up in the world."

The room has an entry with a tiny bubbling fountain. Through the archway, there's a large sitting room. A huge urn filled with brightly-colored, tropical flowers sits next to a balcony, and their floral, almost citrus fragrance fills the air.

Flink's talons tap on the stone floor as we walk inside. He sticks his snout up, sniffing the painfully romantic chamber.

"If you destroy anything, I will be forced to make armor from your hide," I inform him.

He blinks at me, looking innocent as can be. Laughing under my breath, I unclip the lead from his harness.

I pass right through the sitting area, past the balcony with its gossamer curtains billowing in the breeze, off to see if the bedroom—more specifically the mattress—is as grand as everything else, but a knock at the door stops me.

Flink, curious, waits by the entrance, probably hoping our visitor comes bearing gifts of food. Oddly enough, the man does.

"Good evening, my lady." The attendant wears a warm smile that must be taught to all employees upon hiring. "I was instructed to bring you refreshment." Then, nodding to each thing on the wooden tray, he says, "I have chilled cider, espresso, honey cakes, and an assortment of seasonal fruit."

My stomach rumbles despite my earlier resolve to skip dinner. "It looks lovely, but I didn't ask for food to be brought up."

"You are Lady Lucia, correct?"

"I am."

"Then it's yours." His smile never falters. Perhaps they're charmed on all the attendants' faces. "Sent from Lord Thane."

Sebastian must have decided I couldn't possibly feed myself. I hold out my hands to accept the tray. "Well, thank you."

I set the food down on the table by the fountain and rummage in my pouch for a tip.

The man bows in thanks and closes the door. "Pleasant evening."

I glance down at Flink, who's eying the honey cakes with dragonish glee, and gently swat his snout. "Get your nose down. Those will make you sick."

The dragon follows me back into the sitting room and gives me a reptilian glare when I place the tray on a high counter. He can reach it, of course. But he's lazy, and standing on his back legs would require a degree of effort.

Before I leave Flink here so I can search for the bathhouse, I pick at the fruit. I'm just debating which piece to try first when a strange snuffling noise drifts from the only room I haven't explored.

Startled, I look toward the pitch-black bedroom. It's dark outside now, and the curtains are drawn. Flink lowers his head and tail and lets out a soft warning growl. Fruit forgotten, I reach for my bow, glad I didn't leave it with my things, which haven't been brought up yet.

I nock an arrow and creep toward the dark bedroom. I have no free hand to carry any of the lamps which are scattered about the sitting room, so I'm at a disadvantage. Flink nudges past me, taking the lead. Some light shines in from the sitting room, illuminating the foot of the bed. The frame is swathed in netting—to protect against mosquitoes I'm sure, but like everything else in this wretched place, it has a romantic look to it.

Nothing lunges at me as I wait for my eyes to adjust. Once they do, I can just make out the source of the noise. Atop the covers, a man lies stretched out on his side. I shake my head to clear it, sure I'm seeing things. My mind is playing tricks on me—cruel tricks at that. Because the man has a heartbreakingly familiar look about him.

I creep forward, arrow still at the ready, and nudge the sleeping man's foot with my knee. It's probably a misunderstanding, that's all. Somehow the attendant at the desk already assigned this room and forgot to write it in her ledger. It will give the man heart failure if he wakes to find a woman with an arrow trained on him.

Cautiously, I drop the bow but keep the arrow in place. "Sir?" He twitches, and I nudge his foot again. "Excuse me, sir!" I repeat, far louder this time.

Possibly too loudly in fact.

He leaps up, unfortunately out of the slice of meager light shining in from the other room, and groans.

"Who are you, and what do you want?" I demand, my heart racing. I realize there's a chance he's merely a criminal off the street who broke in for a free night's rest, and I raise my bow.

"Ask me a thousand times, and the answer will always be the same," he says in a husky, sleep-heavy voice that makes my heart sing.

Overwhelmed and shocked, I drop my bow. It clatters to the marble floor, and then the room is perfectly silent.

The man steps into the light and strides toward me, a smile growing on his handsome face. "I want you, Lucia."

"Avery," I breathe, not ready to believe it's him. The captain's at sea, still on his way to Marlane. There's no possible way he's here.

"Lucia," he says, his sleepy eyes growing more alert by the second. He lets them roam over me now, and a smirk grows on his lips. "You're not supposed to be here yet."

"Me? You're supposed to be at sea!"

He yanks me against his chest, enveloping me in his arms and the rich, spicy scent of his cologne. The fragrance more than anything tells me this isn't some elaborate dream my brain concocted—my mind couldn't have constructed that smell so perfectly. I sink against him and wrap my arms around his waist, pulling him as close as possible.

"I had an epiphany two days after I set sail."

"And what was it?" I murmur against his chest—which I just now realize is delightfully bare.

He pulls me back, laughing when I reluctantly cling

to him. Not giving in to me, he makes me meet his eyes. "The Greybrow Serpent was needed in Marlane, true. But my crew is more than capable of making a simple pickup and delivery without me. So I turned the ship around, sailed for Montaview's coast, and parted ways with my men, putting Gregory in charge and my boatswain at the helm. Wasting no time, I hopped on a Riverboat, sailed up through Eromoore, and entered into Elrija soon after."

Akello's words from earlier in the street run on a constant loop in my head, but instead of filling me with dread as they did when they were spoken, I feel giddy.

Avery chose me over his ship.

"How long have you been here?" I ask.

"A few days." He raises an eyebrow. "But I didn't expect you yet. According to the map linked to the tracking spell, you're still in Eromoore."

Ashamed, I look at the floor.

He places a hand on my chin and tilts it up so I will have no choice but to look at him. "Lose the dagger?"

"To a harpy."

His eyes widen with surprise, but he laughs. It's the most welcome sound in the world—deep and real and happy.

"I'm so sorry."

Avery shrugs. "Better the dagger than you."

I take a deep breath, drinking him in. "You're here."

His smile grows. "I think we've established that."

"But you really are."

"I really am."

My eyes drift down until I'm looking at his chest.

Feeling euphoric, I brush my lips against his skin. He goes still, probably as startled as I am that I've made a move this bold.

I graze my fingers against his abdomen, brushing them over the hard ridges.

"Lucia," he warns, his voice growing husky again.

"Why are you in my room?" I ask.

He clears his throat. "It's my room, actually. I left orders that they were to send you up as soon as you arrived."

I hum against his shoulder. "That's rather scandalous, don't you think?"

"I wanted to surprise you. Though I hadn't planned to be sleeping when you showed up." He runs the tips of his fingers up my back. "After that, of course, I was going to get you a room of your own."

"No hurry." I brush my hand over the short strands of hair at his neck and meet his eyes. "I've missed you, Captain. And if you haven't noticed, we are quite alone."

"Are we?" he teases, but his tone is dark and delectable.

We've always been so careful to conceal our true feelings for fear of rejection, but now that fear is gone. Avery is mine; he loves me.

And I love him. I have no doubt.

Yet his muscles are tense with indecision.

"Kiss me, Avery." I pull back and meet his light-brown eyes. "I know you're a gentleman deep down, but right now…" I lean forward and whisper in his ear. "I want the pirate."

He growls under his breath and crushes his lips to mine. Elation swirls in my stomach, and I yank him closer. He pulls the pins from my hair, tossing them to the ground without care, and then he runs his hands through the strands, massaging the base of my skull.

I groan with pleasure and flatten my palms against his chest. It's a wicked pleasure, something I've never indulged in though I've seen him shirtless plenty of times at sea.

Avery nudges me backward, and we bump into the urn. It wobbles from side to side before it finally tips, dumping water and flowers all over the marble floor.

"Ignore it," Avery commands, and I'm more than happy to comply.

His lips are insistent, hungry, and his hands leave a trail of fire wherever they touch me. Somehow—and I can honestly say I have no idea how—we end up on the bed. But before we do something foolish, Avery pulls back.

I take a deep, ragged breath. He hovers over me, his arms trapping me in, and his muscles quiver with restraint. My corset belt is gone, lost somewhere in the vicinity of the sitting room, and my bodice is halfway up my abdomen.

"We have to stop," he says, his voice ragged.

I shake my head, trying to pull him back. "A few more moments, nothing more. I'll behave, I swear."

"Says the half-dressed girl lying on the bed." He raises a wicked eyebrow, and I feel my cheeks go hot.

Playfully pushing him aside, I sit up, yanking my

bodice back into place. "All right. We got a bit carried away."

He sits next to me, his thigh pressed next to mine, and runs a hand through his disheveled light brown hair. "Shame the ceremony on the island wasn't binding."

He says it like it's a joke, but there's truth in his words.

I look at him from the side of my eye. "What's the expiration date on that do you think?"

Wryly, he pushes me back to the bed. This time, it's a sweet move. He lies beside me, propped up on his arm. "About six months ago."

"Yes, a shame," I repeat his words, turning so I'm facing him.

Avery runs his hand over my arm, and we fall silent. I close my eyes, enjoying the sensation. There's still heat between us, but it's cooled to a bearable simmer. After a few moments, he trails to my neck and idly wraps the chain I wear around his finger.

I open my eyes, watching him, not daring to breathe.

When he drops the chain, the pendants it carries fall from my bodice, dropping to the bed. One is the charm I wore to keep from getting ill at sea. Its magic has faded, and now it's nothing more than a cheap trinket. But it reminded me of the captain, so I continued to wear it in the desert.

The other is a ring set with a rare sea fire ruby.

His eyes fall on the ring, and a smile plays on his lips. "Have you worn it on this chain since we parted?"

"I have," I whisper.

His eyes lock with mine, and he studies me for several moments. "What if we were to do something foolish?"

I sit up. "Like what?"

He joins me and then slips to the foot of the bed, kneeling at my feet. With his eyes still on mine, he takes my hands.

And my heart forgets how to beat.

"Lucia."

"Avery?" I gulp. A little voice yells at me to keep calm, to not get my hopes up.

"I would like to preface this by saying that I was planning to ask you somewhere wildly romantic—likely tropical, perhaps—"

"Get on with it."

He grins. "But I don't want to spend another night without you. Not one. And there happens to be a charming chapel not two blocks away, complete with a Kalaen bishop..."

Unable to speak because the blood is rushing through my veins so quickly, I only manage to nod.

"Lady Lucia Linnon, would you do me the great honor of marrying me...tonight?"

"Are you serious?" I squeak.

He bites back a grin and leans forward conspiratorially. "Did you forget your line?"

And I laugh because it's Avery. Of course he's not going to do this right—and why would I want him to?

I squeeze his hands. "Yes, Captain Greybrow. I will marry you...tonight."

8

SECOND TIME'S THE CHARM

"I'm sorry," the kindly middle-aged man says. "If the girl has no family to give their consent, then I cannot perform the ceremony."

Avery stands next to me, arm's crossed, looking about as agitated as I've ever seen him.

"Does it have to be my father?" I ask after several moments go by. "Or would my brother be all right?"

The bishop gives me a kind smile. "A brother is fine."

The captain flashes me a look, one I can't quite decipher.

"We'll be back." I'm already dragging Avery from the chapel.

"Might I remind you that all four of your brothers are back in Reginae?" Avery says.

I glance at him. "Not all of them."

Avery stops me in the street. "I know your families have made your relationship with Sebastian confusing, but he's not kin."

61

I grasp Avery's hand. "If he agrees to give me away, are you going to stop him?"

A smile twitches on his face, and he shakes his head, looking out at the street. "No."

"Come on then."

We try Sebastian's room first, and then Adeline's. They're still not back.

"What time is it?" I ask.

Avery pulls a pocket watch from the inside flap of his jacket. "Half past eight."

They should return soon. I can't imagine either of them staying out late. I slide my back down the wall outside Adeline's room until I'm sitting with my legs stretched out in front of me. I pat the cold marble on my right. "Have a seat, Captain."

Avery joins me, and we wait...and wait.

And wait.

My eyes get heavy, and I feel myself drifting. Last time I asked Avery the time, it was fifteen minutes until midnight.

I wake to a loud cry of surprise and blink several times.

"Captain Greybrow!" Adeline exclaims. "You're here!" Then she cocks her head to the side. "But what are you two doing outside my room?"

Yawning, I pull myself to my feet.

"I need to speak with Sebastian." I turn to my business partner—the man I've known my entire life. The only person who knows me better than my own family. "Alone."

Sebastian's gaze goes between Avery and me. "Lucia, it's past midnight. We'll talk in the morning."

"No." I step in front of him, making him look at me. "Now."

He drums his fingers on his crossed arms. "Fine."

Leaving Adeline and Avery to make idle small talk in the hall, I take Sebastian to Avery's room.

As soon as I open the door, I find Flink fast asleep, crashed out in the middle of the floor, with the empty platter and scraps of food surrounding him. He apparently licked up most of the espresso and cider, but the dredges have made a horrid mess.

"Oh, *Flink*," I say under my breath. I wave Sebastian in. "Never mind that now."

Sebastian eyes the suite. "Your room is a bit grander than mine."

"Avery's doing."

"Shocking."

I pin him with my eyes. "I thought you two were getting along."

He shrugs. "Well enough."

"Good, because I need you to give me away so I can marry him at the little chapel we passed on the way to the caravanserai."

Sebastian's eye twitches. "Excuse me?"

"I know what I'm asking of you." I soften my voice and step forward. "But the bishop said I needed someone from my family to give their consent."

"I'm not—"

"You are," I say firmly, not giving him a chance to

argue. "And don't you dare say you aren't."

He shakes his head. "What you're asking...your father will hate me. Your mother will be devastated."

"Or she'll think it's wildly romantic."

Sebastian raises his eyebrows.

"All right, probably not." There's not a romantic bone in my mother's body. "But Sebastian, I love him. And Avery loves me. And in our line of work, you never know what's going to happen next. I don't want to wait."

He paces the room, rubbing his neck. "And yet I distinctly remember you saying this would be the easiest mission of them all. Just a quick trip into the desert and then back home. What's the rush?"

And it will be an easy expedition—I have no doubt. But still.

"Sebastian," I say sternly. "If you care for me at all—if you ever have—you will do this for me."

He turns back. "That's a low blow, Lucia."

"But you'll do it?"

After staring out the balcony for several moments, he closes the distance between us. "Promise me—swear to me—you have thought this through. That you truly want this."

"I have. I do."

He lets out a long sigh and looks over my shoulder. Softly, he says, "I don't know if I can do it."

"Do what?"

"Give you away." He shakes his head and meets my eyes. "Give you up."

I purse my lips to lock in the emotions that swirl in

my chest. I understand; I do. We're a team. We're Sebastian and Lucia. But once I marry Avery, that will change. As it must.

I nudge him with my elbow. "You're not giving me up. You're making us actual family."

And thank goodness, his lips tip in a crooked smile. "Cousins."

"Cousins."

He takes my hand and squeezes it. "Yes, all right."

"Really?" I ask, overcome.

Sebastian nods, though he still looks like he thinks it's a bad idea. "Yes, really."

"Oh, Sebastian!" I cry as I throw my arms around him.

The door opens, and Avery and Adeline walk into the room. Adeline looks taken aback, but Avery gives me a wry look. "Either he agreed, or I should be worried."

I give Sebastian one more tight squeeze, and then I run for the captain and leap into his arms. "He agreed!"

ADELINE FRETS OVER MY DRESS, but I sit in a happy stupor, content to let her do her work. We're in her room, which is where I was forced to spend last night.

Sebastian may have agreed to officially give his consent, but he wasn't about to let me wake the poor bishop at one in the morning.

Now it's almost nine, and I've been up for hours. Actually, I'm not sure I slept at all.

They say a bride is nervous on her wedding day, but I am euphoric.

I barely register Adeline standing in front of me, frowning.

"What?" I finally ask.

"Down or up?"

"What are you talking about?"

She lets out a longsuffering huff. "Your hair."

"Oh." I try to look studious as I think it over, but the grin wins. "I don't care. Do whatever you think is best."

"Do whatever you think is best," Adeline mutters under her breath. She sticks several pins in her mouth as she begins to fuss with the brush. "Your hair has gotten long in the last year," she mumbles through the pins.

"Avery seems to like it."

"Let's leave it down then." She ends up twisting a few front sections up, working her magic. Finally, she steps back and admires her work. After several long moments, she beams at me. "You look lovely."

Then she yanks me up and drags me to the long mirror she had several of the caravanserai attendants bring up.

I, of course, packed nothing that would double as a wedding gown, so Adeline lent me one of hers. It's champagne silk, and the skirt is full. At Adeline's insistence, I wear a farthingale. Today, I barely even notice my lack of air.

My reflection looks back at me, rosy cheeked and bright eyed. I set a hand on my stomach, trying to quell the butterflies.

"You're getting married," Adeline says.

I meet her eyes. "To the captain who robbed us and left us stranded in the wildlands."

She grins, and her eyes brighten with amusement. "Who would have thought?"

Before she can answer, there's a knock at the door.

"Are you ready, Lucia?" Sebastian calls in.

Adeline fans herself with her hand, more nervous than I am. "She's ready."

Sebastian's gaze falls on me as soon as he walks in the room, but he won't meet my eyes. "Avery's waiting for you at the chapel. I'm here to escort you there."

I run a hand down my skirt, self-conscious. "All right."

He doesn't mention the gown or the purpose for the outing, and by the time we reach the chapel, I'm ready to take him by the shoulders and shake him.

A woman who introduces herself as the bishop's wife greets us at the door. She motions Adeline into the chapel, and she escorts Sebastian and me into a small room off to the right. The bishop waits for us there.

I try very hard not to chew on my thumbnail as he asks Sebastian a variety of questions, such as what it was like to grow up with me in Reginae and about family and so on. Thankfully, he never specifically asks if Sebastian is my flesh and blood brother.

It's no surprise that Sebastian breezes through the light inquisition. He knows everything a brother would know, and with detail.

No longer worried, I watch with affection as he

laughs with the bishop after telling the man about one of our misadventures when we were younger.

"And do you give your consent to this marriage?" the bishop finally asks.

I hold my breath, waiting.

For the first time today, Sebastian meets my eyes. "If this is what Lucia wants, then I give her my blessing."

"Thank you," I silently mouth.

Sebastian signs a document, and the bishop and his wife leave us.

Once they're gone, Sebastian digs into his inner jacket pocket. "I picked you up a ring for Avery."

"Oh, thank you," I breathe, taking it from him gratefully. "I completely forgot."

He extends his hand. "Are you ready?"

Tears prick my eyes, and I nod. "I cannot tell you how much this means to me, Sebastian."

"I know."

I accept his hand, but when I expect him to walk me out the door, he tugs me close and wraps me in a tight embrace. "Lucia," he whispers.

That's all he says—just my name. But I know what he means. I squeeze him tightly, hoping to convey to him how much he means to me.

He steps back and clears his throat, wiping any trace of emotion from his face. "All right. It's time."

Without further ado, he tucks my hand through his arm and escorts me into the chapel.

Adeline stands near the front. She sniffs once, and then she loses all composure. Tears stream down her cheeks. The bishop's wife stands next to her and hands her a handkerchief.

I smile at her, but when we reach the front, I only have eyes for Avery. He's in his gray captain's jacket and black breeches, looking as handsome as a man can be. He must have polished his boots this morning because the black leather gleams. As soon as he meets my eyes, he gives me the wicked smirk that I was lost to the moment I saw him.

We reach the front. Sebastian gives me one last long look before he transfers my hand to Avery's, and then he steps down and joins Adeline.

I have a terrible case of déjà vu through the entire ceremony, and flashes of our marriage on the island play in my mind. As if he's feeling it too, Avery's lips twitch.

This time, however, we understand the vows. We know exactly what we're agreeing to.

It passes quickly. There's no reason for show when there are only three people in attendance.

We exchange vows and rings, promise our lives and love and eternal loyalty, and then there is only one thing left.

"Captain Greybrow, you may kiss your bride," the bishop says with a wide smile.

I yank Avery toward me, laughing as he kisses me soundly in front of the small gathering.

And just like that, I am married to Captain Avery Greybrow.

9
DOES IT HURT?

"So how much are we worth exactly?" I ask as I trail a finger over Avery's bare chest.

We lie wrapped in blankets, atop the gloriously soft bed in the caravanserai. The sun obnoxiously decided to rise this morning, announcing that our blissfully short honeymoon is over. I expect Sebastian to come pounding on the door any moment.

We've almost been married seventy-two hours.

Gorin graciously offered us his congratulations upon his return and said we could stay in Stali one more evening. Yancey on the other hand, wasn't impressed the captain returned so early. Or at all. Frankly, I don't expect a wedding present from him.

Avery angles his head to look at me, a lazy smile on his face. "Let's put it this way—if you were to decide you'd like an island of your very own, I could make that happen."

I laugh and snuggle closer. "I wouldn't mind visiting

an island, but I don't need one of my own at the moment."

"That's a relief," he says lightly, chuckling to himself. "The paperwork required for that sort of thing is madness."

Rolling onto my stomach, I prop myself up on my elbows. "What happens when we return to Kalae?"

He stretches, and the light filtering in from the balcony catches the gold highlights in his light-brown hair. Idly, he trails a finger over my back. "We will attend a very tense afternoon tea with my grandmother and sister, an even more intense meeting with your father and mother, and then I'll take you to meet my father. After that, we can go anywhere you want, do anything you want."

"I want to travel for a while. Believe it or not, I rather miss the Serpent." With a sigh, I flop down. "But we have to finish this expedition first."

And like clockwork, there's a knock at the door.

Groaning, Avery crawls out of bed and only pulls on a pair of pants.

"If it's a maid, you'll give the poor girl heart failure," I say as I lounge in the covers, admiring Avery's well-toned upper body. My husband is rather spectacular.

The captain shoots me a smirk over his shoulder and closes the bedroom door, giving me privacy while he attends to our unwanted visitor. In a few minutes, he ambles back into the room and leans against the door-frame. "That was Sebastian."

"You don't say."

"He informed me we have fifteen minutes to pack and get downstairs, or he'll send Yancey in to help."

I laugh and toss the covers back. Avery's eyes stray, and I go warm.

"Later, Captain," I whisper as I step past him to gather my things. He catches me and pulls me against him, delaying us considerably.

An hour later, we meet the rest of our party. Sebastian won't meet my eyes, and Adeline blushes every time she looks at me.

Honestly.

And then I realize they won't look at each other, either. Which is odd—unless something happened between them last night. Maybe I'll corner her later and ask about it.

"Did you find what you were looking for?" I ask Yancey, since he's the only one not acting strangely.

"Yes." He frowns at Avery. "Did you?"

I purse my lips, trying to hold back my glee, and then say, "I believe so."

He rolls his eyes.

We're saved from the conversation by the attendants bringing our trunks and luggage out on carts. An hour later, we're riding out of Stali, into the desert, toward Struin Aria. It's been two weeks since Gorin found us in Teirn, and we still have two and a half months of spring left. Even though it will take several days to reach the ruins which contain the map, we will have plenty of time to retrieve the lily. Simplest mission yet.

I'm in high spirits, even atop my donkey. But that

doesn't stop me from glancing over at Avery. "Why do you get a horse?"

He gives me a knowing look. "I brought him with me."

"Yet your bride rides a donkey."

"And she looks adorable."

I try to hide my smile. "How about a trade?"

Laughing, Avery shakes his head. "Not a chance."

MY DONKEY PLODS along at a sedate pace, trotting down hills and lumbering up the next. This is our third day of the expedition, and so far, I believe we are making decent time. This part of the desert is desolate, and the ground is cracked. The soil is so alkaline, there are places where the dirt is crusted with sheets of mineral. It looks like frost. Occasionally, there is a scraggly ballo bush, but we haven't seen any animals since leaving the plains outside Stali.

And it is hot. So very, very hot. Adeline rides behind Sebastian, covered from head to toe in skirts and scarves to protect her fair skin from the desert sun. I fear she must be roasting. Every so often, she fans herself, though it doesn't do any good. There is no respite from the heat.

"Are we going to stop for lunch soon?" Adeline calls to Gorin when the sun is high in the sky.

Gorin appears hesitant to stop, so I add, "I'm hungry as well."

Our guide frowns and nods, and we find a spot that

has a cluster of boulders large enough to sit on. I fall from my donkey, groaning as my feet hit the ground. Sebastian leaps down and helps Adeline from their mule. Though she doesn't announce how sore she is, I can tell she's as glad to be off their beast as I am to be away from mine.

Gorin passes out parchment packages of honeyed sweet rolls and spicy dried meat. I settle onto a rock next to Avery, guarding my parchment when my husband playfully eyes my roll. Starving, I eat quickly, and when I'm finished, I rest my hands behind me and turn my face toward the sun.

Flink wanders from person to person, begging for scraps. I haven't confirmed it yet, but I have a suspicion that Yancey tosses him treats when no one is looking. The dragon always seems to linger near him.

Content with Avery by my side, I idly listen to my companions' conversations.

Adeline asks Gorin how much longer we will ride today, and Yancey complains to Sebastian that he's been away from the guild for over two weeks now, and we haven't needed his services once. Avery adds things here and there, but I am content to listen.

Drowsy in the sun, I lie back on the rock, toss my hands over my head, and close my eyes. I'm just drifting when a sharp, stabbing pain wakes me. I yelp and leap up, clutching my wrist. The burning sensation is bright and hot, and it spreads all the way to the tips of my fingers and up my arm.

Avery stands with me, his brow etched with concern. "Lucia, what is it?"

He tries to look at my wrist, but I yank it back to my chest, woozy with pain. Concerned, his eyes move to the rock where we were just resting.

"Gorin!" Avery yells. "What do you know of the native scorpions?"

Going pale—an admirable feat for one as tan as Gorin—our guide rushes over and looks at the spot where Avery points. The culprit scurries across the boulder, as unrepentant as a creature can be. Gorin sags with relief when he spots the huge, shiny black scorpion. "It's all right. It's just a rock creeper."

"All right?" I demand as I hold my wrist, practically bent over in pain. Tears prick my eyes, but I don't care. The world spins, and I can barely stand.

Avery wraps his arm around my stomach, supporting me.

Gorin nods, sympathetic. "It hurts like all oblivion, but their sting isn't fatal like their cousins."

"And what do those look like?" Sebastian asks, frowning at the villainous arachnid.

"They're smaller, and the tip of their stinger has a brown line that runs up their abdomen."

Sebastian turns to me. "Does it hurt very much?"

Does it hurt?

From the look I give him, he figures out the answer on his own and wisely backs off. He turns to Yancey. "Do you have anything you can give her?"

Yancey ambles over and yanks my arm without

bothering to ask permission first. Heat—not the pleasant kind—races through my arm, and it takes every ounce of willpower I possess not to punch him in the face.

"On a scale of one to ten, with ten being the worst, where would you rate the pain?" he asks, almost sounding bored.

I rip my arm away and snarl a curse that shouldn't be repeated in polite conversation.

Our alchemist nods, his grim expression twisting into a morbid smile. "Rather high then."

"Can you do anything?" Avery asks.

Yancey shrugs. "I believe so, but it'll take me about an hour to whip something up."

"I'm fine," I say through gritted teeth. I will be soon anyway. "Let's move on."

Avery seems hesitant, perhaps because my wrist is turning purple, and he turns to Gorin. "How long will it take to subside on its own?"

Gorin rubs the back of his neck, thinking. "A day... maybe two?"

I stumble forward, and Avery clasps my shoulders.

"Better make her something," Sebastian says.

Yancey nods as if to say, "suit yourself" and pulls a long, wicked-looking dagger from the sheath on his hip. Then, without ado, he stabs the scorpion. Once it's skewered on the blade, he carries it away.

Adeline, who's cowering atop her mule for fear of touching the ground, follows the creature with her eyes, looking pale and horrified.

Unable to stand any longer, I fall against Avery. "You know—I don't feel so well," I mumble.

Sebastian touches my shoulder, saying something, but my mind is too clouded with pain to pay attention. And just like that, I pull an Adeline and pass clean out.

"How's your wrist?" Avery asks as he nudges his horse next to my donkey.

I glance at the lingering red mark on my skin. Yancey packed a poultice around it yesterday, which I remember nothing of. In fact, all I do remember is waking to the foul-smelling gunk on my arm and five pairs of anxious eyes, looking down on me. Well, Yancey didn't actually look that worried. Put out—absolutely. Worried—not so much.

"It feels fine," I assure Avery quickly, cutting off the conversation before my business partner overhears and brings it up again. All day, Sebastian's teased me mercilessly about passing out.

Slowly, we make our way toward a towering mountain range that's dry and rocky, but more visually appealing than the rolling hills.

Gorin trots forward, looking at ease on his mule. "Ahead are the Tairan Mares."

"That mountain range there?" I ask.

He nods. "It's nasty territory—snakes, spiders, the occasional imp. Best be careful."

"You have imps in Elrija?" I ask. We have the flying

nuisances in the mountains of Reginae, and I'm not keen to run into any here. "Do they carry an element?"

The ones at home sneak up behind you, and if they are successful, they'll grab you by the shoulders and send a jolting wave of magic coursing through your limbs. Once you're down, the nasty thieves will steal anything of value. Their shock is rarely fatal, though I have heard that the young and elderly are more susceptible.

"Just desert imps," Gorin answers, not terribly concerned. "And I've never let one get close enough to find out if they're elemental."

Our group laughs, but I honestly couldn't care less about the imps. My mind is preoccupied with the other creatures he mentioned.

"What about the snakes?" Avery asks knowingly, catching my eye from atop his horse.

"I've seen both rock vipers and copper cobras along this trail." He directs his next words at Avery. "The mules are less likely to spook than your horse, so you best be careful."

"And the donkey?" I ask.

"She's as solid as a rock," Gorin assures me.

I glance down at my "rock." Her long ears twitch, and her head bobs with her uneven gait. She does seem rather unflappable.

I roll my shoulders, already tense.

"Nervous, Lady Adventuress?" Avery asks, his eyes bright and his tone lighter than usual.

"No."

"So you're not scared of snakes?" He raises his eyebrow.

"No."

The captain urges his horse closer. I focus on the reins in my hand and not on how near he is. I had no idea what torture this expedition would be, but it's excruciating. Avery and I are together, which is a blessing, but we must keep our distance for the sake of the group. Being this close makes my blood hum, and from the look in his eyes, I think he knows it.

The captain leans down from his horse and taps my bow. "Think you can shoot one?"

"Shoot what?" I ask, distracted.

He laughs. "A snake."

I glance at him and raise a brow. "What do you think?"

Along with his usual enchanted broadsword and several daggers, Avery's strapped a bow of his own on his back, along with his sword and several knives. The portable arsenal certainly looks good on him. Reaching behind him, he pulls several arrows from his quiver. "Perhaps you should have these, just in case."

I gape at the lovely arrows—the lovely *glowing* arrows. "Avery…" I whisper.

He flashes me a quick grin. "Thought you'd like them. I saw them in Stali and thought of you."

And without another word, he leans down, looking as if he's going to tumble right from his horse just to reach me on my little jenny, and transfers the arrows to my quiver.

"Thank you," I say.

He rights himself and nods, his eyes warm. "Think of them as a wedding gift."

The trail begins to climb, and we are forced to move forward in a single-file line. Flink ends up in front of me, trapped behind Adeline and Sebastian. He doesn't seem to mind the position, and he trots along happily, often stretching his wings in the sunshine like a great, scaled butterfly.

I keep my eyes on the terrain around us, peering into dark crevices and holes, wondering if the slithering menaces are lurking. As we climb the dry, rocky mountain, the path narrows. I stare at the ledge uncertainly, but my little donkey doesn't mind—doesn't seem to even notice—and she plods along at her usual, slow pace.

Occasionally, she takes a wrong step and stumbles slightly. I hold on to the reins for dear life, praying nonstop that we'll reach the summit soon.

"Are you all right, Lucia?" Gorin calls from the lead.

I gulp. "Fine, thank you."

"No passing out again," Sebastian adds.

I glare at the back of his head.

When nothing horrific happens, I finally find the courage to look at the canyon to our left. It's not all that deep, not compared to other places I've traveled, but it's quite the sight with its towering sandstone formations jutting from the ground. Now that we've left the foothills, the earth has gone from mineral-devoid tan to rich red, and there are occasional veins of dark, oily shale.

"Rock viper to your right," Gorin calls to our group. "It's sunning on a rock not far from the trail, but as long as you make no sudden movements, it should let us pass."

It's just a *snake*. A small, element-less, measly little snake.

And though I try not to look, I catch a glimpse of it as we grow near. Its scales are red and tan like the cliffs, and I'm not sure I would have seen it if Gorin hadn't pointed it out. The wretched creature watches, alert. Its head slowly bobs from left to right, and its *nasty* little black tongue darts in and out of its *nasty* little snake mouth, and my heart nearly stops. Gorin passes unscathed, and then Sebastian and Adeline do as well.

"It's fine, Lucia," Yancey assures me from behind Avery. "If it moves, I'll push it back."

And yet again, I'm reminded that I need to learn a little wind magic. I wouldn't worry about the viper at all if I knew I could harmlessly nudge him away with a simple gust of air—or toss him off the cliff. Whichever.

Just when I think we're going to make it through without an incident, Flink stops dead in his tracks and focuses on the viper, forcing my donkey to come to an abrupt stop.

"Flink, no," I hiss.

Completely ignoring me, the dragon cocks his head to the side, studying the snake.

"Flink!" Not wanting to spook the viper, my words are no more than a whisper, but Flink certainly hears them. His haunches twitch, and his wings flutter with anticipation.

Height temporarily forgotten, I twist on my donkey's back. "Yancey!"

But before our alchemist can assist, Flink lunges.

10
BEST KIND OF DISTRACTION

The snake rears back and then springs forward in a fluid, graceful movement that spooks my stoic mount. The donkey brays, startled, and stumbles back. She bumps into Avery's horse, who decides to correct the situation by nipping my little jenny right on the rump.

She screams and leaps forward. I have a death grip on my reins, trying not to squeal myself.

Everyone's hollering at once. Flink's battling the viper, and my donkey is dancing far too close to the edge. Though it seems like several minutes, it's only a matter of moments before the snake goes limp in Flink's jaws. I somehow calm my donkey, though don't ask me how, and she stops making that awful noise. Then I take several deep breaths, trying to calm *myself*.

Flink, quite proud of himself, holds the snake up, looking suspiciously like he's going to bring it to me.

"Don't you *dare*."

His golden eyes flicker with confusion, and I feel bad for half a second. But Flink looks away, giving me the dragon version of a shrug, and then the horrid beast *eats* the snake. He literally slurps it right up, and the tail disappears into his reptilian mouth like an errant noodle. I think I'm going to be ill.

Adeline makes a disgusted noise ahead of me, and her face twists with revulsion, likely mirroring my own.

"All right," Gorin calls from ahead. "Let's keep moving."

I exchange a look with the dressmaker, and then she turns back to Sebastian, facing forward, and we continue our slow trek through the Tairan Mares.

"Gorin," I holler ahead after another not-so-close encounter with a desert viper. "Will we make it past the range tonight?"

The trail has meandered away from the cliff, and I feel more at ease now that there's a quarter mile expanse between us and the canyon. Red sandstone monoliths rise around us. Half our trail is over vast stretches of smooth slickrock. Patches of crunchy black moss grow on the surface of the sand like a thin crust. I've never seen anything like it in my life.

"No," Gorin answers. "But I know a good place to stop for the night."

The last of the sun's golden rays stain the western sky when we arrive at the camp. A charred circle of rocks and forgotten graying ashes betray that we are not the first to take shelter at this natural crevice in the rock wall. Nearby, there is the sound of bubbling water, and Gorin and Avery already lead their mules to it.

We climbed high enough that the spring air is chilly. I dig my cloak from the very bottom of my saddlebag and look around. There are even evergreens at this altitude. Granted, they are scraggly, sad-looking specimens, but they are honest to goodness trees nonetheless.

Nearby, Sebastian tries to coax Adeline from their mount while she adamantly swears she is far too tired to move a muscle. Though he knows full well she's exaggerating, he doesn't see it for what it is—a desperate attempt to get him to take her into his arms. *Honestly.* He's the smartest man I know, and yet sometimes he's as dull as a post.

But then something passes between them. Their eyes stay locked a moment too long, and they share a secret smile. Maybe he's not so dull after all.

Smiling to myself, I turn to gather wood for the fire.

"You look very serious," Avery leans close and whispers into my ear.

I smile but stare into the fire. "That's because we're keeping watch."

The moon is high in the sky, and according to Avery's pocket watch, we're nearing the end of our shift. Everyone is sound asleep in their tiny tents. Even the mules are quiet.

"I have people for this sort of thing." He loosens my

hair and brushes it behind my shoulder. "Perhaps you should tell me how it works."

"Well, generally the people on duty are supposed to pay more attention to their surroundings than each other." My heart picks up its pace as Avery runs his fingertip down my neck.

"Keeping watch sounds boring," he whispers, and his lips follow the trail his finger just took.

Trying not to smile, I squirm away and pull my cloak tighter around my shoulders. "You are the worst kind of distraction."

"Then I'm not doing it right," he murmurs, his lips moving to my ear since he can no longer access my neck. "I was rather hoping I'd be the *best* kind of distraction."

"Avery—" I say, turning my head, about to tell him to behave himself.

Before I can, he threads his hands through my loose hair, holding my head firmly but gently, and stares at me with a cocky but sweet expression on his face. "Has anyone told you that you're beautiful in the moonlight?"

"Has anyone told you that you're a pest?"

He flashes me a quick grin. "Would you say pest is below or above pirate?"

Unable to help myself, I shift closer to him. "They're fairly equal."

"You know where this is going to end." He leans close enough his body blocks the chill of the cool night, and his words tickle my lips. "Why not give in now and save yourself some time?"

"You are a bad man, Captain Greybrow."

He slides his arms around my waist and yanks me closer, nearly taking my breath away. "I like the sound of that."

"And what if the camp is attacked by desert imps while we're distracted?" My hand strays to the laced neckline of his lightweight, muslin shirt. I wind the rough leather tie around my finger.

"They'll carry Adeline away, and Sebastian can play the hero. It's a win-win situation." He nips at my bottom lip, which effectively steals every last ounce of my common sense. "Tell me anything Adeline would like more."

Unable to help myself, I laugh and move in to tease my lips against his. That's all the invitation Avery needs. His hand tightens at my waist, and I pull him closer.

His lips are a hot contrast to the cold air, and the shadow of stubble on his jaw tickles my skin. It's deliciously wrong, considering we're on watch, and I cannot get enough.

"Lucia," he breathes after several long, blissful moments. "We should probably—"

I gasp for breath and then yank him back. "Stop talking."

He groans in agreement and deepens the kiss, pulling back just enough to murmur, "If you insist."

The smell of the night surrounds us—the sharp scent of the scraggly brush, the crisp emptiness of the desert air. Even the sandstone gives off a rich mineral fragrance of its own. It's so quiet, so perfect.

The only noise on the breeze is the far-off sound of a

donkey braying. Which is strange, considering we haven't seen a soul in days.

I end the kiss abruptly and pull back. "Did you hear that?"

"No." Avery pulls me back.

Distracted, I turn my head. "I heard a donkey."

"I don't care if you heard a rockslide." With a hand to my cheek, he tilts my head and kisses the sensitive skin in front of my ear.

I listen for several moments, but there is nothing else. Shrugging it off, I meet Avery's kiss, taking no time to deepen it again.

"I've decided I like night watch," Avery says against my lips.

Just as I'm about to answer, a sharp, shrill shriek fills the night and echoes off the nearby canyon.

Avery and I leap to our feet. Our movements are clumsy since we're both half-delirious. My cloak falls off my shoulder, and Avery's shirt is askew. We blindly reach for our weapons and run for Adeline's tent.

Sword drawn, Avery barges through the flimsy fabric with me at his heels.

A man stands hunched over, just inside the tent, and Avery lunges for him. The man ducks just in time.

"Stop!" Adeline cries. Simultaneously, she casts a light spell, which illuminates the small space and the four people who barely fit in it.

"Sebastian!" I cry, my heart racing. "What are you doing?"

I can hear Gorin and Yancey rousing outside.

Sebastian stammers, and he looks very much like he wants to crawl into a viper hole. Instead of answering me, he turns to Adeline. "I couldn't sleep. I just wanted to talk."

She stares at him, wide-eyed. Even disheveled, she looks lovely. It's unfair, really.

"All right," she says, her voice breathy though she tries to hide it.

Avery and I glance at each other, both amused and irritated that they scared us half to death.

Sebastian, acutely aware of our presence turns his gaze on us. Dryly he says, "How's the watch going?"

He must have seen us.

It's our turn to look embarrassed. Well, *my* turn. Avery seems smug. "Fabulous, actually. I will gladly volunteer to do a watch every night."

"Perfect," Sebastian answers. "Tomorrow you can partner with Yancey."

As the men poke at each other, Adeline shoots me a look, telling me to get out.

I take the captain's arm. "Well, since everything's all right—"

A wicked look crosses Avery's face. "Yes, we'll gladly give you some privacy."

Adeline makes a frazzled sound that's either a giggle or a noise of distress. Sebastian has the decency to look chagrined, but there's a smile playing at the corners of his mouth.

"So you can...*talk,*" Avery adds, wiggling his eyebrows suggestively, just to be rotten.

If I don't get him out of here, Adeline will never speak to me again. I yank the captain's arm and shove him from the tent.

"Everything's fine," I say brightly when we find Gorin and Yancey lingering outside.

Avery gives them his charming smile. "Adeline had a nightmare, but fear not—Sebastian's taking care of it."

Yancey rolls his eyes.

"All right," Gorin says, amused. "You two can get some sleep. Yancey, you're on the next watch with me."

They wander to the fire to take their posts. Once we're alone, Avery looks at me and raises an eyebrow. "Do you anticipate nightmares?"

I step close and toy with his collar. "I don't know, Captain. Maybe you should stay with me?"

"Gladly," he growls and pulls me into our tent.

I'm not sure we're going to get much sleep tonight.

II

ARRIVE AT DUSK

Struin Aria looms in the distance, a city forgotten. Like Stali, the buildings are clay. Slightly higher on a hill, a fortress overlooks the city. It alone is made of white stone, decorated with ornate, crumbling balconies. It stands like a forgotten bride. A feeling of emptiness has settled over the valley.

I find it incredibly eerie, but somewhere in there, we'll find the map that will lead to the lily. And the sooner we collect it, the sooner we may return to Kalae, and then back to the sea.

I glance at Avery, remembering our time on the island in the whirlpool. Maybe we'll find another deserted island, somewhere secluded and lush. Just the two of us.

He catches me looking, and a slow smile builds on his face. I bite the inside of my cheek and look away.

"The wells are tainted, right?" I ask Gorin, getting down to business. "That's why the city was abandoned?"

"That's right." Our guide nods to our alchemist. "But that won't be a problem with Yancey here."

And though he'd like to hide it, Yancey puffs up under Gorin's praise, even if all he'll be doing, as he put it, is "boiling the water."

Shadows grow as the sun sinks behind the distant hills. The city is protected by a wall, and the only way in is through the massive iron gates—gates that stand wide open. I eye them as we pass through, half expecting something to jump out at us.

I glance at Adeline, and she too looks spooked.

We pass abandoned houses with shuttered windows. They're dark on the inside, but a fanciful part of me wonders if something stares back at us. Just as an involuntary shiver travels up my spine, a loud howl echoes in the street ahead of us.

Adeline yips in fright, and Yancey jumps in his saddle. The mules shy, startled as nothing more than a scrawny cat darts down an alley and out of sight. Even my little donkey looks uneasy.

Gorin turns in his saddle to grin at us. "You five all right?"

Yancey glares at him, and I place a hand over my heart, willing it to slow down as I laugh. All that over a cat.

Our party is quiet as we follow Gorin through the city. Fortunately, he seems to know where he's going. We traverse a winding cobblestone road that begins to climb. Soon, we're looking over the city. My unease grows as we ride past the castle fortress's walls.

Gorin dismounts in the courtyard, and we follow his lead.

"Do you want to set up tents or sleep inside?" he asks.

Avery and Sebastian share a look and glance around. It's really a matter of what's the least of two evils. There's something about the city that makes me feel as if it doesn't want us here—or worse, it's eager for our arrival. Which is ridiculous, I know. I'm not usually this fanciful. But this place...

I shiver.

Adeline ends up answering for us. "I don't want to sleep in there."

We all nod in agreement.

"Tents it is," Gorin says, sounding a touch too enthusiastic.

By the time we make camp and eat a meager dinner, the sky is as dark as ink, and the stars are on display. There's not a cloud to be seen, and the night is moonless. Gorin points out constellations to Yancey and Adeline, who both grew up with an entirely different set in Mesilca.

The fire flickers, and its warmth goes a long way to soothe my nerves. The wildlands, with its amphibious beasts and exploding seed pods, were far worse than this. Yes, the city is a bit unnerving, but at least nothing has attacked us. Yet.

Adeline holds out her hand, letting a turquoise flame flicker in her palm. I watch her, mesmerized. "What are you practicing?"

"Sleeping charm," she says. "I'm trying to decide if I can perform it on myself. Otherwise, I'll never rest tonight."

Sebastian smirks. "I can do it for you—I'm getting good at it since you taught me. I used it on the harpies." He flashes me a wicked smirk. "And I performed it on Lucia after the scorpion stung her."

I gasp, pointing a finger at him. "I knew I didn't pass out!"

The group laughs, breaking some of the tension around the camp.

After a while, my eyes grow tired, and I yawn behind my hand. Exhausted after the last few long days of traveling, I lean against Avery and close my eyes. *I* certainly won't need a sleeping spell tonight.

"Are you ready for bed?" he murmurs in my ear.

"Mmmhmm," I mumble back.

He says something else, but there's a new sound on the breeze—a rider. I sit up, now awake. Sebastian too narrows his eyes, listening.

"What is it?" Adeline looks at Sebastian.

"Sounds like we have company," Gorin says, but he must not be expecting any of the good variety because he pulls his bow from his pack.

The rest of us stand alert, arming ourselves with our weapons of choice—Avery with his ancient enchanted broadsword, Sebastian with his rapier, Adeline with her meager magic, and me with my bow. Yancey doesn't need a weapon; he strikes a menacing stance, which is enough to make the most menacing of villains tuck tail.

"They're approaching," Gorin says quietly as he draws his bow. I too nock an arrow and wait.

Avery steps behind me and whispers into my ear, "Is this a bad time to tell you how ravishing you look?"

"Probably," I answer with a smile.

I only hear one animal, and it's in no hurry. It seems as though we wait forever. Finally, the rider crosses through the cut in the wall. He rides a donkey no larger than mine and wears a veil over his head and face. With his long, lean legs, he looks like a giant on the small creature, and I fleetingly wonder if I look ridiculous on my little jenny as well.

Perhaps startled to find us on guard, the man yanks his mount to a stop. The creature dances sideways from the shock.

Gorin swears under his breath and lowers his bow. "*What* are you doing here?"

I too let my bow drop, but I keep the arrow nocked because Gorin's tone doesn't sound terribly friendly.

The rider pulls away the head wrap, unleashing a cascade of riotous curls and a shockingly pretty face. "I've come to help."

Gorin glares at the girl. "And what did my brother have to say about it?"

She swings down from her donkey, giving it an affectionate pat before she leads it to our group. "I didn't ask."

"Esme—"

"Stop right there." She strides toward him and pokes him in the chest. She's tall—only a few inches shorter than Gorin. She'll tower over Adeline and me. "I am a

95

year older than you. Therefore, you cannot order me about."

Gorin's nostrils flare, and he pulls his eyes from her to address the rest of the group. "This is Esme." He hardens his eyes and looks back at her again. "My niece."

Niece? She just said she's older than Gorin.

Instead of flinching under his scowl, she runs her fingers through her hair, trying to tame the light-colored curls, and then sets her hand on her hip and gives us a carefree smile. "Pleasure to meet you all."

Her eyes run over us, and then they pause on our alchemist. Slowly, her gaze rises to meet his. "You're tall."

Expressionless, Yancey studies her. "As are you."

"What's your name?"

"Yancey."

She snorts out a brief laugh. "That doesn't suit you."

He crosses his arms, unimpressed.

"I like to refer to him as The Boulder," I offer.

Esme turns to me and grins after she sizes me up. "You're Lucia? The adventuress? Aren't you a little...slight?"

My, isn't she honest.

"Sometimes feisty things come in small packages," Avery says, feeling the need to defend me.

It's the captain's turn to fall under Gorin's niece's scrutiny. A smile plays on her lips as her eyes rove over him. "You're a handsome one."

"Esme—" Gorin begins, flustered.

"Taken," Avery says before Gorin can finish. To prove his point, he puts his arm around me.

Her answering laugh is friendly, and she finally turns to Adeline and Sebastian. "What about you?" she asks my partner. "Are you taken as well?"

This has the potential to go very, very badly. I tense next to Avery, wondering how my idiot friend is going to reply.

Adeline stares at Sebastian intently. He glances at her, unsure how to answer. She gives him a full three seconds before she makes a disgusted noise and disappears into her tent.

Esme raises her eyebrows but stays thankfully silent. Sebastian rubs a hand over his neck, murmurs his apologies, and hurries after Adeline.

"I've been trying to catch you for the last several days," Esme ends up saying to Gorin.

"I must have heard you in the canyon while we were in the Tairan Mares," I say.

"Probably. I was sure I almost had you that night, but I couldn't find where you were camped." She laughs. "And then I got lost."

Gorin clenches his jaw and looks up at the sky.

"But I found my way."

"Did you bring a tent?" Gorin asks. "Supplies?"

She shrugs. "I have everything I need."

"I'll take that as a no." He glances around and frowns. "I suppose you'll have to share with Adeline."

Before I can tell him that's a downright foolish idea, Esme shakes her head. "I'm fine, Gorin. Stop being so overprotective." And with that, she flips her hair over her shoulder, digs a lantern from her pack, lights the wick with the dying coals from our fire, and walks into the fortress. "I'm going to explore. I'll see you all in the morning."

Gorin looks downright livid, but he bites back his frustration and turns to us remaining three. "We're protected from the desert here. I don't think there's need for a watch. Let's all get some sleep."

Avery and I retire to our tent. Wrapped safely in his arms, the abandoned city doesn't seem so unsettling. I'm just drifting off when I hear voices carrying from the city below. I roll over to face Avery. "Did you hear that?"

"Hear what?" Avery mumbles, almost asleep.

I listen again, but there is nothing but silence. I must have been half dreaming. Either that, or Gorin, Sebastian, and Yancey are still awake.

"Never mind," I say as I cozy up closer to him. He wraps his arm around my waist, tucking me close, and I let myself drift.

"Lucia," Sebastian hisses from outside the tent. "You need to get up."

I blink and groan. The courtyard floor was entirely too hard, and my back is sore. Avery mumbles next to me and draws me closer, trying to fall back asleep.

"Avery, you too."

Growling, Avery sits up and stretches his shoulders.

He peers at the light. Judging from what's filtering in the tent, it's far too early to start the day unless you're a bird.

We throw on clothes, and Avery yanks the tent flap aside. "What could possibly be so important that you have to wake us at the crack of daw—"

He goes quiet, and I nudge my way past him.

Apparently not *all* birds are starting their day.

"Whose idea of breakfast is *that?*" I ask, disgusted.

Five dead crows lie in a circle around the fire ring, all facing the same direction. I won't lie; it's a wee bit disturbing.

"It's a warning," Gorin says. He stands with his arms crossed and a dark look on his face. "Something doesn't want us here."

I step closer, looking at the birds. "I don't care for the way you say *something*."

"It's an ancient Elrija saying—an old wives' tale," Gorin explains. "Five crows in a ring, death it will bring."

Sebastian glances around the camp, searching the ground for tracks. Finding none, he turns back to the fire pit. "We need to get rid of them before Adeline wakes up."

Yancey hasn't said anything since I left my tent, but he kneels to remove the poor birds. Just as he's reaching for the first one, Esme strolls from the fortress.

She looks different in the early light of dawn. Her long, tightly-curled hair is lighter than I thought—honey blond, and her complexion is a warm, dark tan and as flawless as a young girl's. From this distance, I can't tell what color her eyes are, but they look light. She's exotic and positively stunning.

"Good morning," she says brightly, and then she frowns when we only murmur our hellos. "Sour bunch you all are before breakfast."

Then she sees the crows. Her eyebrows shoot up, and she takes a step back.

Gorin looks up, half-livid. "If this is your idea of a joke—"

"Excuse me," she hisses. "*That's* not amusing in the least. How could you accuse me of this?"

His expression falters, and then he looks down. He rolls his shoulders, trying to release the tension. "No—you're right. I'm sorry. But if it wasn't you, who did it?"

We end up looking at each other, waiting for someone to shed some light on the situation.

When no one has an answer, Yancey resumes his task, taking the birds far from our makeshift camp. Adeline joins us in a few moments, and on Sebastian's request, we pretend nothing is amiss. We don't mention the birds at all.

12
SERPENTS OF ELRIJA

"Lucia, I think I've found something," Sebastian hollers from down a hall.

I pick up my torch, leave the room I've already gone through twice, and follow his voice. Gorin claims the map's *supposed* to be somewhere in the castle fortress, but the place is a lot bigger than it looks.

We've already wasted three weeks, and we have nothing to show for our time. So much for an easy expedition.

I find Sebastian leaning over an old desk, studying a thin leather sheet.

My heart leaps, and I race forward. "Did you find it?"

"Not exactly." He turns the old leather so I can take a better look.

Squinting, I hold the torch closer and turn to my partner. "It looks like a map of this castle."

"It is." He points to an alcove in the very center, near the main entrance. "But what's this?"

I study it and nibble my lip, thinking. "I have no idea. Why haven't we found it?"

"I think it's been sealed off. Remember the mosaic in the hall?" He points to its approximate location, which just happens to be where the map shows the door to the alcove. "Doesn't that look like a place where a door once stood?"

A tiny flicker of excitement lights in my belly. Somehow, I know he's right. "We should show Gorin."

We hurry through the fortress, trying to locate the others. Avery's off "exploring," which is a Greybrow codeword for treasure hunting. He's already found a passel of artifacts to bring back home, including a couple impressive enchanted blades. The captain's like a young child in a confectioner's shoppe.

Gorin and Esme are working in a lower level where a combustible fuel was stored in urns. Since they didn't dare take a torch, Gorin requested Adeline's magical services.

Yancey's outside, not being the slightest bit helpful. He poked around a bit on the first few days, but then he grew bored.

We reach Gorin's underground storage room, but it's empty.

"Adeline was complaining of a headache when I saw her earlier," I say to Sebastian. "They probably went out for fresh air."

After looking around for another fifteen minutes, we make our way outside. Adeline's in the shade of a pillar, resting her head against the stone. Sebastian kneels in front of her. "How's your head?"

She opens her eyes, gives him a sweet smile, and waves his concern away. "The dust and fumes got to me, but I'm feeling better now."

I look around for Gorin. He, Avery, Yancey, and Esme share a packet of dried meat. We've had the same thing for weeks now. I can barely stomach it anymore—even the smell makes me queasy.

"We found something interesting," I say to Gorin.

His eyes light. "What kind of interesting?"

Sebastian comes up behind us and spreads the map out on the makeshift table Yancey constructed last week when he was exceptionally bored. Sebastian tells them just what he told me, and by the end, they're nodding.

It takes the men no time to gather an assortment of picks, hammers, and one immensely large ax, and then they gleefully head into the fortress to do some damage. Even Yancey volunteers to be of assistance this time.

I follow, ready to demand someone hand me a tool so I can assist, when a bout of nausea overwhelms me. I set my hand on the wall, willing it to pass.

"Lucia?" Avery asks, setting his pick aside. "Are you all right?"

"I didn't eat this morning," I confess. "Or this afternoon."

"Tired of dried meat?"

"So tired."

He chuckles and retrieves his pick. "Let's break this

door down, find the map, and ride to the closest city for a real meal."

The entire party enthusiastically agrees. Unfortunately, the picks aren't doing the job.

"We're going to need something stronger," Yancey finally says. He wipes the sweat from his brow and tosses his hammer aside. "I think it's spelled."

Sebastian nods. "It must be."

"What do we do?" Adeline asks from beside me.

We all stare at the wall, thinking. Finally, Gorin heaves his pick aside. "It's getting late. We'll return to it in the morning."

Murmuring our agreement, we leave the tools behind, ready to return to them tomorrow.

As Gorin starts a fire, I settle on the ground next to Esme.

"So Gorin is your *uncle?*" I ask her as the tinder ignites.

Esme glances at me, amused by the question. Her eyes are tawny—so rich a brown they are gold. Almost catlike. They give her a mischievous look, and I haven't decided yet whether they are misleading. "Yes, and yet I am eight months older."

"How does that work?"

"My grandmother was very young when she had Father…and very old when she had Gorin."

She smiles to herself as she looks out over the city. It's not yet dusk, but it will be shortly. The light is still golden, and it shines down on Struin Aria, making it look friendlier than it is.

Esme goes to take a drink from her waterskin, but it's empty. "Do you have any more water, Yancey?"

He searches for the bucket where he's been keeping the cleansed supply, but it's missing. He looks this way and that, and finally, Sebastian clears his throat and points to the middle of the courtyard. Flink sprawls in a muddy pool of his own making. The bucket lies empty beside him.

"Wretched beast," Yancey snarls as he stalks toward the dragon. Before he can reach him, I run ahead and snatch the bucket from the ground.

"I'll fetch more from the well," I tell him.

He looks like he wants to argue, but he finally nods and walks back to his newly constructed table to set up his alchemy supplies.

After a moment, he asks, "Where's the map?"

Sebastian and Avery stop mid-conversation and turn toward Yancey.

"It was right there," Sebastian says.

Yancey gestures over the empty table. "It's not here now."

An uneasy silence blankets the group. We haven't had anything strange happen in weeks, not since the crows. I think we all tried to put it behind us.

Unable to bear the tension, I start walking. "I'm going to the well."

My proclamation must startle our party out of their silence, because they begin to murmur amongst themselves.

The wind probably blew it away. No reason to jump to conclusions.

I've been to the well several times, and I'm not usually as uneasy as I was that first night. But tonight... tonight I feel as if someone—or something—is watching me.

I quicken my pace and reach the well just as the sun sets. There's still plenty of light, but I'm spooked. I fight with the crank, which decides this evening of all evenings is the time to stick. Finally, I hook the bucket to the latch and lower it into the water.

I'm just cranking it up when I hear the strangest noise behind me. Before I turn, there's a whir of air, and an arrow sinks into the soft wooden frame, inches from my head.

I gasp and step back, dropping the bucket into the well. But it's not just an arrow; there's a map attached to it. *The* map. And written across it in black, dripping letters is a warning. I whirl around, hoping to find the archer before he disappears.

Instead, I find three cobras.

My stomach leaps to my throat, and I freeze. The black and bronze serpents watch me, already agitated. Their hoods are raised, and they weave back and forth, scenting the air with their tongues. They are huge, far larger than I would have guessed. Their bodies are wider than my fist, and the largest is several yards long.

What am I going to do? I don't have a weapon, and what good would it do me anyway? As soon as I went for one snake, the other two would attack.

I stay as still as possible as I think my options over. I can only see one outcome—I'm going to die.

Just as I'm debating leaping into the well, something startles the snakes. They whirl their heads around, looking down the street I just came from. Their eyes dart back and forth, keeping an eye on me as well.

Avery steps into view, followed by Flink. "Lucia, I thought I heard—" He goes as still as me, his eyes widening when he sees the cobras. "*Don't move.*"

Do I look like I'm going to?

Flink spots the snakes moments later. Avery realizes the dragon's intentions seconds too late. He tries to grasp Flink's harness, but the dragon is too quick. Flink darts for the snakes, weaving back and forth like a cat wary of its prey.

Deciding the dragon is the greater threat, the serpents turn from me.

I back around the well, careful not to draw their attention again.

"Give them a wide berth," Avery warns, his eyes on the snakes.

Flink lunges for one but leaps back when the second attacks. They're fast, but he's faster. And he appears to be enjoying himself.

The dragon makes his first kill, and the other two cobras attempt to retreat. He lunges at the second, and then finally, he kills the third.

My heart beats wildly in my chest, and I feel as if I'll never draw in a full breath again. As soon as Flink vanquishes the threat, Avery rushes toward me. He frantically runs his hands over my shoulders and down my sides, checking me over.

"I'm all right," I assure him once I can speak.

"Thank goodness for Flink." His voice is low, and I know the encounter rattled him.

"I'm fine—just a little shaken, I promise." I wish there were a way I could assure him more, but even if there were, I know he's not going to take the next part well. "But, Avery, there's more."

I point to the arrow.

His mood changes in an instant. Before, he was worried, perhaps a bit regretful he wasn't the one to save me. But now he's livid—the kind of livid that should make that archer hope the captain never finds him.

Avery rips the map from the arrow and reads the words aloud. *"Five crows in a ring, death it will bring."*

On the map, right over the ancient cartography, encircling the warning, are five sketched crows.

Avery slams the parchment on Yancey's table, making the whole thing shake, and he glares at Sebastian. "We found your map."

Yancey scrambles to right his wobbling equipment. He's about to holler at Avery, and then his eyes narrow on the warning scrawled across the leather.

Before anyone can comment on it, Flink strolls into camp. The largest of the cobras, his prize, is clamped in his jaws, and its tail drags behind him like a banner.

Esme gasps and leaps back. "That's a bronze cobra!"

Adeline scrambles away as well, but Gorin takes a step closer, his forehead knitting. "We're too low. They live higher, in the Tairan Mares. It shouldn't be here."

"Yet him and two of his companions found Lucia," Avery snarls.

Gorin flinches at the captain's tone.

"We must scout the city, see if we can find who's responsible for this." Avery steps toward Gorin, his expression hard and unyielding. "But when we get back, you have some explaining to do."

We split into two groups. Yancey comes with Avery and me, and the rest go with Sebastian. I feel far more confident with my bow on my back and one of Avery's new blades at my side. We search until dark, but we never see a sign of the archer who dropped off my slithering gift.

Hours later, we sit around the fire. Not surprisingly, no one's eager for bed tonight.

Sebastian leans forward, resting his elbows on his thighs. "Surely you can think of some reason why someone would want to stop the expedition."

Gorin stares into the flames and shakes his head.

Avery, who's still furious, points at Gorin. "If you do not give us some explanation as to why Lucia was attacked, I will take my wife, and we will go back to Kalae."

Sebastian nods. "I'm sorry, Gorin, but I agree."

Gorin buries his head in his hands. "I don't know

why someone would be bent to stop us from finding the lily—I truly don't."

"Gorin's beloved, Falene, is the princess," Esme blurts out, taking us all by surprise. She glances at Gorin, apologetic. "Her father, the man dying of the aging disease, is our king."

We sit quietly for several moments, processing the information.

"You fell in love with a princess?" Yancey asks, incredulous. "Wishful thinking."

Esme shoots the alchemist a stern look. "She's not a princess. She's *the* princess—King Azel's only child. And she loves Gorin as much as he loves her." She lowers her voice and stares at the ground, resolute. "Even if it's foolish."

Gorin holds up his hand.

"Enough, Esme." He rubs his neck. "My mother died when I was only ten years old. My father and Josef, my brother—Esme's father, were in Kalae with their caravan at the time, and I had to live with my aunt until they returned for me. Aunt Alexandra worked as a companion for Falene, and she brought me along. The princess and I became friends.

"Half a year later, Father returned, and I left with them. I didn't see Falene for years, might have forgotten her if she were not our princess. But every time I went to the king's city, I'd look for her." His voice grows wistful. "I'd see her occasionally on the balconies."

He goes quiet, but we wait, knowing there must be more to the story. Finally, he clears his throat and continues, "Last year, Josef had a delivery for the king himself, and I begged him to let me take it. On the day, I wore my best clothes and bathed twice—I was a wreck. And I wrote her a letter." He shakes his head, smiling at the memory. "She wasn't there. I crumpled the note and tossed it in a bin on the way out. Crushed, I left. As I was weaving through the city streets, a girl cried out to me. I turned, and there she was, running past the vendors, hair streaming behind her, shining in the sun."

"Had she seen you? Did she remember you?" Yancey interrupts, slightly more invested in the story than I would have expected.

Gorin shakes his head. "No, but she found my note."

"What did it say?" Adeline whispers.

"That I've never forgotten her. That I watch for her whenever I'm in Kysen Okoro." He swallows, and though it's too dark to tell in the firelight, I'm positive he's blushing. "That she's beautiful."

"And she saw you toss it away as you left?" Adeline says.

Gorin nods. "She said she was curious what could make a man look so dejected. We reconnected that afternoon, and I know it sounds mad, but I promise you I fell in love with her that day. A week later, I took a job in the palace. Ten months after that, the second-born prince from Guilead came to Elrija and asked for Falene's hand. The king accepted."

"So how did we get from that point there, to searching the desert for a map leading to a lily while an unnamed someone tries to kill my wife?" Avery asks, but his tone is lighter than before.

"A few weeks after King Azel made the agreement with the Guilead prince, His Majesty began showing signs of a bizarre aging illness. He's not an old king, but his hair went white in a month. Then he began to ache, and his joints became stiff. Soon, there were wrinkles around his eyes, and even more on his hands. He already looked fifteen years older.

"Falene came to me, desperate. She begged me to find the lily, said it was the only thing his physician believed could save him. I agreed—of course I did. I would do anything for her. But she took it a step further. She led me to her father, right into his throne room, and told him that if I did this, if I saved him, in exchange, he would let us marry."

"And he agreed?" Adeline asks.

"Not at first. Three days went by, and then the illness grew worse. Azel began to have trouble rising, and walking became a chore. Finally, he accepted Falene's bargain." He holds out his hands in a placating gesture. "But I have no idea why someone would come after us— I swear it. I didn't know I was putting you in danger." He meets my eyes. "Lucia, I am so very sorry."

And I believe him.

Sebastian stands, thinking. "The way I see it, we have two possible scenarios at play. The first is that someone wants the king dead. Who's in line for the throne?"

Gorin shakes his head. "Falene has reached majority, and Elrija allows the crown to pass to a female heir."

"Does anyone else hold a grudge against Azel?" Sebastian asks.

"Not that I know of. He's a good king. People are fond of him—as fond as one can be of their ruler, anyway."

"Then that leaves this prince of Guilead."

Avery nods as if that's what he had been thinking as well.

"Daniel? He wouldn't wish the king dead," Gorin argues. "The prince is kind and reasonable—once Falene explained our relationship, he supported us, said if we could find a way to be together, he would step back."

Sebastian and Avery exchange incredulous looks, but they don't press further.

Yancey doesn't choose the same tactic. "He was willing to hand over the opportunity to rule Elrija as a prince consort? I'm sure any man would give up that sort of power so that he could be thought of as 'kind.'"

Esme leans forward, locking her eyes with Yancey. "Cynical, aren't you?"

"I prefer rational."

I hold up a hand. "I'm afraid Yancey has a point, but let's stop here for a moment. There is another option we haven't discussed."

The group turns their attention to me.

"What if this isn't about the king or the princess or Gorin at all." I pause and glance out at the darkened city. "What if someone doesn't want us snooping around the fortress?"

"Why?" Adeline asks, uneasy.

The feeling I had when we first arrived in Struin Aria

returns, settling around my shoulders like a clammy hand. "I have no idea."

"Well, if that's the case, let's get out of here quickly." Yancey stands. "Gorin, what kind of fuel was in the room you scouted today?"

Gorin sits back, surprised by the abrupt change of subject. "The liquid variety imported from the far west—the type the wealthy cities used to run through underground rooms before the art of light magic was understood."

"I don't suppose there was any sparking powder?" Yancey asks, speaking of a powdery mined mineral most often used to start cooking fires when wood is slightly green or damp.

Our guide thinks about it for a moment. "There might have been. Why?"

A satisfied—and slightly terrifying—smile spreads across Yancey's face.

13
NOT A GOOD SIGN

It's nine in the morning, not one of us got a lick of sleep, and Yancey is playing with explosives.

"You're sure this is safe?" I ask him as I watch him work his alchemy magic.

He mixes powders and fuel, adds a little heat, and infuses it with magic until it smokes. "Not likely."

I suppose that's the only answer I could receive when he's making a combustible powder that he's trying to blend just perfectly. Get the wrong concoction, and his plan won't work. Too much and he'll blow the entire fortress down.

"When did you learn to do this?"

"Journeymen alchemists learn in their second year." He frowns at the powder, which has now changed to an alarming bright orange.

I think about his answer for a moment. "But you're still a novice."

"That's right."

"So how did you learn?"

He adds a few pinches of this and that. "I read ahead."

Help us all.

Looking like a gleeful child, he glances up. "Have no fear—I know what I'm doing. This is the reason I got into alchemy in the first place."

Well, that makes sense. I always wondered what it was about the plant magic that intrigued Yancey. Now I understand—he wanted to blow things up.

"Finished," he proudly proclaims. Then he meets my eyes with a wicked look on his face. "Now we must test it. Where's your dragon?"

I narrow my eyes. "If you even think—"

He clamps a meaty hand on my shoulder as he rises. "It was only a joke, adventuress." He grins. "Lighten up."

I gape after him as he collects his orange powder and takes the road into the city. Fifteen minutes later, the ground shakes, and a massive cloud of fire engulfs one of the deserted cottages below. Gasping, I stumble back.

The fool blew himself up.

Avery and Sebastian waste no time. They run down the road after Yancey, expecting the worst. Five minutes later, the trio returns, laughing like they haven't a care in the world.

"It worked!" Yancey yells. His face is black, and his hair is singed. I'm not sure he has any eyebrows left.

Esme steps next to me, looking irked. "Men are strange. What is their fascination with fire?"

"I have no idea."

She storms over to Yancey, smacking him in the chest. "Are you mad? You could have killed yourself!"

I glance at Adeline, and she tries to hide a smile. We've noticed something these last few weeks. Yancey and Esme fight…a lot. Perhaps a little too much.

Carefree and as sooty as a chimney sweep, Yancey slings his arm over Esme's shoulders. She looks taken aback, probably unused to being around someone taller than she is. "But I didn't kill myself. Now, if you'll excuse me, I have a mosaic to decimate."

I step up next to Avery. "Who thinks giving Yancey this sort of power was a bad idea?"

Avery laughs. "I don't think any of us gave it to him. He took it and ran."

We follow the others into the fortress, though I think we're all a little reluctant to do so. Yancey fusses with his powder for several long minutes, and then he packs wet clay around it and adds a long bit of string he dipped in melted wax.

"What's that for?" Gorin asks.

"It's a fuse," Yancey says. "I'll light it and run."

I give Avery a pointed look.

Moments later, Yancey shoos us outside, instructing us to go to the edge of the courtyard, at least. We stand about, waiting. Several minutes go by, and then a few more. We're all growing anxious when suddenly, Yancey runs from the door, darting faster than I thought a man of his stature could travel.

He's almost to us when a loud boom sounds from the fortress, and a cloud of dust and smoke comes billowing out the entry. When the smoke clears, shards of broken mosaic, clay, and who-knows-what-else lie scattered on the ground.

Yancey claps his hands together, his eyes bright and slightly unhinged. "Who's ready to find the map?"

The dust is still heavy when we step in. I cough and wave my hand in front of my face, trying to clear it. As Sebastian suspected, just past the great gaping hole in the wall, lies a room we have yet to explore. Avery's the first to venture inside.

Soon, all seven of us are inside. Adeline casts a light, and it hovers over us, illuminating the tiny space. The alcove is square in shape, not very large, and there are a few upholstered benches and a small table. A hundred years of dust layers the furniture, and there's a damp smell to the air.

"Who would block off a sitting room?" Sebastian muses as he looks about the room.

Gorin walks to an old bookshelf and starts poking around. Adeline checks a drawer in the table.

I sniff the air, and Avery nods in agreement. "Mildew."

"Where's the water coming from?" I ask.

The room itself appears to be dry.

"Look for a hidden door." Avery kicks a rug aside and then grins in a self-satisfied sort of way. "Or a secret hatch."

"I've had enough of those," I say, referring to the plethora of underground tunnels we found in Teirn this winter.

"Come on, darling," the captain coaxes playfully. "Don't you want to know where it leads?"

The wooden door sticks at first, but he finally pries it open.

Adeline cranes her neck to see into the dark pit. There are no stairs leading down, only an ancient ladder. "I don't particularly need to know," she says.

"I'll go first," Gorin volunteers. Once he's down, he yells up, "It's not too deep."

Sebastian goes next, followed by Adeline and her light.

Avery gestures for me to go. "After you. Unless you'd like me to go first?"

Fortunately, dark, dank rooms don't bother me. I climb down and take in the dim surroundings. Once Avery's joined us, we wait for Yancey and Esme to stop arguing about who's going to go next. Esme eventually wins.

We're in a wide tunnel, and though it's not damp yet, the area feels musty. Adeline's light reflects off the stone walls, revealing webs made by creatures I have no desire to run into.

"Ready?" Gorin asks once we're all down.

Adeline peers at the ceiling. "What do you think is down here?"

"Vermin, spiders, snakes—"

"That's enough, Avery," Sebastian snaps when Adeline looks like she's going to crawl right up that ladder and take our light with her.

Avery flashes me a mock-innocent look.

"Where are we at exactly?" Esme asks.

"Under the fortress," Yancey answers, just to rile her.

"The map didn't show this area," Sebastian says before they start bickering again. "We'll just have to look around."

"Is it safe?" Adeline takes a not-so-subtle step closer to Sebastian.

"Most likely," Sebastian assures her.

We make our way down the tunnel, looking for offshoots. As we walk, insects scurry away from Adeline's light. Fortunately, the tiny crawling creatures are the worst thing we've found.

"It looks like there's a door ahead—" Gorin leaps back just in time. A huge ax falls from a crevice in the wall, swinging pendulum-style in front of us. Its blade glints in the mage light, and it goes back and forth, eventually losing momentum.

"Good thing you moved in time," Avery says lightly despite the deadly trap in front of us. "Otherwise, you would be half the man you were when we started."

Esme snorts, but Gorin shudders.

"Too soon?" Avery whispers to me, his eyes bright.

"Maybe a little."

Cautiously, Sebastian angles around the blade, keeping watch for pressure plates on the floor. "Someone went to a lot of work to keep people out of here. There's a plaque on the door, something ancient."

"What does it say?" I call to him.

He shakes his head. "I have no idea. It's in Rilcreal."

"I can read it." The captain steps over the blade as if it were nothing more than a log in the road.

Sebastian rolls his eyes and steps aside. "Be my guest."

Avery pulls his reading spectacles from his pocket, and I do my best not to swoon. I love him in those glasses.

"Danger," he reads. "Beware of..."

The captain squints and rubs his sleeve over the plaque, trying to work away the dust. Half the wood crumbles.

He looks at Sebastian and shrugs. "It's rotted."

"Beware of what?" Adeline squeaks.

"How long ago do you think they sealed the alcove?" Gorin asks.

I glance around and then inspect the blade. "I think they closed it off long before they left the city. What do you say, Sebastian? Two hundred, three hundred years ago?"

Sebastian nods. "That sounds about right."

"Let's say they did lock something nasty inside," Gorin continues. "What could have survived two hundred years? Trolls only live to be a hundred or so, goblins fifty. What's the worst thing that could possibly be behind that door?"

Avery nods sagely. "A very ripe troll corpse."

Adeline's light flickers.

"You know you're going to open it," Yancey says. "Hurry it up so we can get out of here."

"What's wrong, Yancey?" Esme teases. "Scared of the dark?"

I step away from them and join Sebastian and Avery. "What do you say?"

Avery shrugs, but Sebastian looks resigned. "You know it's locked."

"Well, my friend, I just happen to be prepared for exactly this sort of occasion." Avery pulls out a familiar pouch.

"You have a lock pick kit," Sebastian deadpans.

"You never know when it will come in handy."

"Obviously."

Avery pulls out a few picks and jimmies the lock. Just when he almost has it, he glances over his shoulder. "We're sure we want to do this, correct?"

Sebastian and I exchange a long look, and then I ready an arrow. The others arm themselves as well. "Open the door."

The lock clicks, and Avery pushes the door open. It swings effortlessly, nearly silent. I wait, barely breathing, unsure what to expect.

There is nothing but the unnerving sound of leaking water. After several moments, Sebastian nods for Adeline to join us in the front.

Cautiously, looking like a terrified bunny, she shuffles forward. Her light flickers and dims, and then it goes bright again. She must be trembling.

"Stay close to me," Sebastian says. "Lucia, behind Adeline."

Avery takes his place at my side, and we creep into

the room. It's a long rectangle, with stairs leading down to a sunken area in the middle. I have no idea how far they go because a pool of water has collected at the center. In a perfect rhythm, the water falls.

Drip. Drip. Drip.

Goosebumps rise on my arms, and a crawling sensation travels my spine. I gulp down my nerves, sure they're from the many warnings and not from the premonition of danger itself. After all, what could possibly leap out at us in this ancient, dark, wet room?

An icy breeze caresses my neck, and I jerk around, looking for its source. Next to me, Avery startles as well.

"Did you feel that?" I barely whisper.

Adeline's light continues to quiver.

My imagination takes over, and I see movement in the shadows, just beyond the black pool of collected water—just past the mage light.

The others are right behind me, but I feel something else. It presses on my skin like a vapor, like icy tentacles, testing...*tasting.*

"I don't think the map's down here," I say as my brain whirls madly to process the sensation. It's bringing back a memory—no, not a memory—remembered stories. Legends. Myths.

Nightmares.

We need to go. We must lock the door, see if we can close off the alcove.

Just as I'm opening my mouth to give my companions a warning, an ear-piercing shriek echoes through the chamber, just as horrid as a siren's cry.

"Wraiths!" Avery yells, but he's too late.

The ghostlike beings rise from the water, ethereal and deadly. We stumble for the door, but it swings shut, locking the four of us inside. Gorin and the others yell on the outside, but there is nothing they can do. We are separated. No matter how I pull on the door, it won't open.

Adeline's light gutters out and then springs to life, like a candle drowning in its own wax.

"Keep it going, Addy," Sebastian cries as he throws a knife at one of the monsters. It's like slicing a cloud—his blade goes right through it and lands with a splash in the pool. "It's the only thing keeping them at bay."

Silently thanking Avery, I nock one of my enchanted arrows and shoot it at the specter. The creature hisses once, but I know we're in real trouble when it passes through, just like Sebastian's knife.

How do you kill a ghost?

The wraiths surround us, trapping us in a circle, moving slowly like a snake squeezing its prey.

"I don't know if I can," Adeline gasps. Her light surges, but just as quickly, it falls dim.

One of the creatures dares to move forward, grasping at my arm. Its cold fingers cut right through me, and I cry out and yank back. It lets go, not daring to come into the light.

"We need more, Addy," Sebastian begs. "Everything you have."

"It's all I've got!" she cries.

The light grows dimmer by the moment. The room

fades, getting darker and darker, until it's dim enough one of the ghost-creatures decides to make a bold move. It lunges into the weak circle of light, wrapping itself around Sebastian. It drags him from Adeline's light, into the pool.

I try to run after him, but Avery holds me back. "Don't be a fool! They'll take you too!"

My partner yells and flails in the water, trying to free himself. The wraiths go mad with sick, morbid glee.

Adeline shrieks, and the heartbreaking sound is as deafening as the keening wail of the monsters. And then the struggle stops.

"SEBASTIAN!" Adeline cries.

But there is no reply.

I fight Avery. When that's no use, I stumble into the captain.

Sebastian.

Suddenly, the room flashes with light as bright as the sun itself. And in that moment, Adeline's wails become something entirely different. She lets out a battle cry, a guttural yell that says she will not lose Sebastian.

The abrupt switch from almost complete darkness to bright, hot light brings me to my knees. I cover my eyes, shielding them, but the light penetrates my eyelids and the arms I have over my face.

Around us, Adeline's scream is replaced with the dying cries of the wraiths. It's a horrible noise, something that will haunt me every time I close my eyes.

And then it goes silent.

I dare open my eyes, and I find myself on the floor,

crouched in Avery's arms. Adeline stumbles to the ground, spent. Her light barely glows, a candle in a ballroom, but the wraiths are gone, and the room no longer carries their cold, dead essence.

Sebastian lies gasping at the side of the pool, soaking wet. He looks up, coughing, and his eyes lock with Adeline's. He crawls for her, and she stumbles for him. He yanks her close, holding her so tightly I'm afraid she might break in the fragile state she's in.

"You did it," he practically gasps as he looks at her with fierce affection. "Adeline—you saved us."

She nods, tears streaming down her cheeks.

And then he kisses her. It's not a sweet kiss—not gentle or hesitant, but the kind that's a long time coming. The kind that comes from near loss.

Avery meets my gaze, still breathing hard, and raises his eyebrows. "About time."

Before I can answer, the door bursts open and Yancey comes barreling in like an angry bull. He stops short when he sees the threat has been vanquished.

"Where did they go?" he asks, stunned.

Avery rises to his feet, and then he offers me his hand. "Adeline toasted them."

"That was *you*?" Yancey demands, looking at the seamstress.

She nods, overwhelmed.

He gives her an approving look, one that says he's impressed—which is like receiving a parade from anyone else.

Gorin leans against the door frame, looking ill. I turn to him. "I don't think the map is down here."

He waves the concern away as if it's the last thing on his mind, but then he hangs his head, perhaps acknowledging that we came down here for nothing. "I know."

"I'm so sorry, Gorin."

"We'll worry about it later. Are you all right?"

I glance at Sebastian and Adeline, who are still clinging to each other. "I think we will be."

14

TIME TO LEAVE

Avery lounges in the shade of a pillar on the edge of our dusty camp. "Who's put it together that it's the wraiths that tainted the water supply?"

I glance at him as Esme wraps my wrist, horrified. "You don't really think that, do you?"

Sebastian wrinkles his nose. "The collected water isn't all that deep. After all these hundreds of years, it should be flooded. It must be leaching into the aquifers."

After the words are out of his mouth, he shudders, likely remembering his time in the wraith's clutches.

Esme and Yancey have already tended his wounds as best as they can using a salve Yancey whipped up once we returned to camp. The pair makes a good team when they're not fighting with each other. Now Sebastian's arms and neck are covered in wrappings to cover the angry raised ice welts that gradually rose on his skin.

I glance down at my own small wound. It aches with

a vengeance—making me a little ill. I cannot imagine
how awful Sebastian must feel, but he's hiding the pain
well—which is to be expected considering he's had years
of practice concealing his emotions.

I thank Esme and stumble to my feet. "I need to lie
down."

Avery turns to me, his easy expression now etched
with concern. "Are you all right?"

I nod and set a hand on my rolling stomach. "Too
much excitement."

"Have you eaten?" he demands, leaving his shady
spot to join me.

I choked down a little of the awful dried meat this
morning, and I tell him as much.

"You've never minded it before," he says, frowning.

"I'm just so sick of it, Avery." I wave his concern
away. "We were attacked by wraiths, and we've been up
for thirty-six hours now—I'm tired. I just need to rest for
a bit."

He walks me to the tent even though I insist I'm fine.

"Adeline's resting," I remind him. "No one's
badgering her."

"Adeline just pulled every ounce of magic from a half
mile vicinity."

"So she's allowed to sleep, but I'm not?"

Avery's eyebrows shoot up, probably surprised at my
sharp tone.

"I'm sorry." I rub my hands over my face. "But please
go away so I can sleep."

He takes me by the shoulders and brushes his

thumbs over my skin. "I don't think less of you, Lucia. I was only concerned."

I nod.

"You promise you're all right? The wraith didn't harm you more than you're letting on?"

"I'm fine. Honestly."

"All right." He brushes a kiss over my forehead and nudges me into the tent with a grin. "Why are you still talking? Go lie down."

Gladly.

But rest must not be in my future because the moment I stretch out on the bedroll, there's a great ruckus outside. Yancey begins screaming at my dragon. Did Flink have to choose *now* to come back to camp?

I stay here for a moment, debating whether or not I'm going to pretend to be asleep, but I know I haven't been in here long enough for that. Just as I rise to my feet, there is a horrible crash, and now *everyone* is yelling at Flink.

I scramble out of the tent and come to an abrupt stop. Yancey's table is on its side, and his supplies are scattered on the ground. Flink's running about the camp, chasing a tiny *something*. Everyone stands on the edges, yelling, but no one bothers to stop him.

"What is it?" I holler to Gorin.

"Sand lizard," he calls back. "Stay back—they're poisonous."

Of course they are. Is there any creature in this wretched kingdom that isn't?

The lizard finally runs into a small crack in the outer

wall, losing Flink. The dragon paces back and forth, hoping it will be foolish enough to run back out.

"Lucia!" Yancey turns to me, livid. "Do you see what your beast has done?"

I look at the supplies. One glass beaker is broken and another is chipped. The rest of his precious explosive powder is scattered on the ground, as are many of his dried herbs.

"I'm sorry, Yancey."

What am I going to do with Flink? We can't keep on this way.

The alchemist must be able to tell how sincerely I mean the apology because his expression softens. "That was all my tinroot powder—I can't purify any more water without it."

Gorin looks ill. He turns away from camp, walking down the road that leads to the city. Esme glances at me, gives me a soft, bolstering look, and hurries after her uncle.

Sebastian turns to Yancey. "How much water do we have left?"

Yancey walks to the bucket—the one he had to fish out of the well. It's high on a wall in the shade where the dragon hopefully can't reach it.

"I have enough to fill each of our water skins, but that's about it. We have to leave today."

He doesn't look as happy about it as I thought he would. I guess after everything, it seems a waste to leave without finding the map.

I help gather Yancey's supplies off the ground, and

Avery leans down to assist. The captain pauses when he picks up a faded book with a worn leather jacket. "What's this?"

Yancey looks over. "I found it inside. It's an alchemy journal. I thought I'd look at it, but with the cobras, wraiths, demon dragons, and adventuress who dropped my bucket in the well, I haven't had a free moment."

"Is it in Rilcreal?" I ask, taking it from the captain. But when I flip through it, I find it's in the common language of the kingdoms. It must not be as old as it looks.

Leaving the mess, I stand. There are a lot of recipes, but also the alchemist's notes—his experiences, where to find specific ingredients. My heart starts to beat wildly. The sketches are beautiful and simple, and I flip through it madly, stopping at all the flowers.

When I find it, I almost drop the journal. "It's in here," I breathe. "This is *the* alchemist's journal."

Avery's at my side in an instant. I bat his hands away when he attempts to steal the journal from me to take a better look himself.

"*...lost the map I copied from the pillar,*" Avery reads over my shoulder. "*I think it blew out of my pack when I crossed under the dragon bridge on the way out of the village. Hopefully, I will find my workroom in one piece when I return. Wretched Kalaen soldiers had torn down half of it by the time I escaped.*"

I turn to Sebastian. "When were we at war with Elrija?"

He shakes his head. "Not for centuries."

"This can't be that old."

We study it for a while longer, but none of us is familiar enough with the kingdom to guess at what the man is referring to.

Eventually, Gorin and Esme return.

"Gorin!" I yell. "We've found something."

He runs forward, almost tripping in his haste. He snatches the offered journal from my hand and frowns as he reads the text. "Dragon bridge," he muses aloud.

"Do you know what he's talking about?"

Gorin shakes his head. "I don't, but this is a good start. At least we have some clue what we're looking for. Once we figure out what village he was speaking of, we can find the original map."

After letting Adeline sleep for another hour, we pack up camp, load the mules and donkeys with our supplies, and gladly leave Struin Aria.

"Where are we headed?" I ask Gorin once the abandoned city is well behind us.

"Malka is a large city on the Elrijan river, and we should reach it by tomorrow. Their scholars' guild houses one of the largest libraries in the kingdom. Hopefully, we can find information on the village with the dragon bridge while we're there."

"Will we have enough water to make it?"

"There's a creek that runs down from the Tairan Mares. It's a bare trickle in most seasons, but it should be running this time of year. We'll camp there for the night."

"How far?"

"Not very."

And thank goodness. We're all half-dead. Adeline's fast asleep, slumped against Sebastian's back. Avery's far too quiet, and Yancey and Esme don't even have the energy to bicker.

Just when I think we won't make it any farther, tall, green trees appear in the distance. I blink several times, not certain I should believe my eyes.

"Gorin, I think I'm hallucinating," I call to him as I ride slumped over on my donkey. "Those look like trees."

"Those are trees, Lucia. The creek is right ahead."

I'm so tired, I could cry. My stomach has felt off all day, and I want to sleep for the foreseeable future.

Flink runs ahead of us and burrows into the soft, silty soil by the water. Finally, we too reach the trees. They are tall, with strong, stout trunks and crinkled bark. Their leaves are large and grow in clusters from small branches, casting the ground in lovely shade.

I slide from my donkey, already dreaming of blissful sleep.

There's little conversation between us as we set about our tasks. Before the sun even sets, we're in our tents.

Avery lies next to me, murmuring goodnights against my neck, and then he falls right to sleep. Nothing feels better than our bedroll and the lumpy ground. Idly, a thought drifts into my head as I feel myself falling. *Is anyone on watch?*

Before I can worry over it, I'm already out.

15
CITY OF LANTERNS

"Maybe they weren't stolen," Avery says wryly. "Perhaps they went for a morning walk."

I glare at my husband, not in the mood for his particular brand of humor at the moment.

The mules, Avery's horse, and both the donkeys are missing. If it's not one thing, it's ten others. My easy expedition is getting more difficult by the day.

Flink's gone as well, but since he's gotten into the habit of wandering, I'm not too concerned about him. At least not yet.

Gorin sits on a tree stump, his head in his hands. He hasn't spoken all morning.

Esme stands with Yancey, looking like she wants to lighten the situation but has no idea how. "This is a popular stop for the caravans," she finally says. "Someone will be by soon, and we can travel with them."

"How soon is soon?" Yancey asks.

She wrinkles her nose. "A week, maybe two?"

135

Adeline is handling the news surprisingly well, but she looks nervous. "How much food do we have left?"

"Enough for half a week," Sebastian answers. "A few days more if we're careful."

I hold up my hand. "I volunteer to give up my share."

Avery flashes me a stern look. I smile like I'm joking, but the truth is, I'm starting to get anxious. I've felt off for days, and even after a full night's rest, I'm still exhausted. This morning I was ill as soon as I woke up. Luckily, I managed to sneak out of the tent without waking Avery. I don't want him to worry, but I'm afraid I might have contracted something.

Though I hate to, once we're in Malka, I'm going to have to find a healer. If we ever make it, that is.

Flink returns early in the afternoon and finds a spot to nap in the shade.

The rest of us are restless.

Yancey spent the morning organizing what's left of his supplies, and Adeline's been working on a handkerchief all day. Avery and I hike up the creek so we can have a few moments to ourselves. Flink wanders with us for a while, and then he gets bored and goes off to do whatever it is dragons do in the desert. He's probably hunting snakes and lizards. There's no denying he's taken a liking to them.

We find a small waterfall and rest in the spray. I'm sullen, melancholy. If we'd gotten on Avery's ship fifteen minutes sooner, Gorin would have never found me, and we wouldn't be stuck in the middle of the desert, hoping for a passing caravan to rescue us.

"I'm about done with Elrija." I watch a giant dragonfly settle on a tall reed growing by the creek.

Avery catches my arm and pulls me over to him. I settle on his lap and put my arms around his neck. We haven't had enough of this time, just us. We've been married for a month, and the only time we're alone is at night.

"I miss you," I say quietly, rubbing his neck.

He angles back, groaning softly as I work the tense muscles. "I know."

"Can we walk to Malka? This waiting will drive me mad."

"It wouldn't be wise to leave our water source, not when caravans pass through here on a regular basis."

"So cautious," I murmur as I lean down to kiss him. "Very *unpiratelike*."

He chuckles and deepens the kiss. We're in no hurry, have nowhere to be, and we might have found the only pleasant spot in the entire kingdom. The creek bubbles over the ledge, and a cool breeze passes through the leaves overhead.

"Lucia," he says as his lips stray to my neck.

"Hmmm?"

"Do you plan to stay in business with Sebastian once we return to Kalae?"

I pull away and look at him. "We haven't talked about it, but I don't know how it would be possible when we'll be at sea so often."

He winds a loose strand of my hair around his finger. "Won't you miss it?"

"Oh, yes." I give him a pointed look. "I love finding myself stranded in the middle of a kingdom that has made it known several times it doesn't want me here."

"I want to be a partner."

It takes me several moments to process what he said. "Avery?"

"I want in on the business, officially. Believe it or not, I bring a lot to the table." He leans forward conspiratorially. "Did you know I have a ship?"

"I heard that somewhere." I straddle him, getting closer. "Do you really want this? Or are you doing it for me?"

"Yes—to both."

"I see how it is," I say, teasing him to cover up the fact that my insides are all warm and squishy, and I'm in dangerous territory of saying something sappy. "You only married me so you'd have an in."

"Naturally," he says in a mock serious voice as he pulls me closer and nibbles behind my ear. "Now enough talking."

"So, we arrive at the port, and Yancey's there, looking like a blacksmith, acting all important," I say to Esme. "Anyway, Flink, who hadn't settled on his element yet, hiccupped a tiny, harmless flame, and Yancey went ballistic."

Esme's laughing, but Yancey scowls. "I don't look like a blacksmith."

"You do," Esme says, swatting one of Yancey's beefy arms.

"Anyway, he's talking big to Sebastian, and *I'm* trying to convince Sebastian to back down—"

"Riders," Adeline says softly.

I turn to her, not sure I heard her right. "What?"

"Riders," she says again, this time louder. Her gaze is fixed in the distance, and she leaps to her feet, dropping her embroidery in the sand. "Look!"

Story forgotten, I follow her. And she's right. It's a medium-sized group, not large enough to be a caravan, and they have no carts.

Adeline waves her hands frantically, trying to get their attention. Gorin rushes over, attempting to stop her. "Adeline, don't! We don't know anything about them."

"What do we need to know?" Adeline demands. "We've been stuck here for four days—four days, Gorin!"

Whether Gorin thinks it's a good idea or not, the riders see us. They change direction, coming our way. Their horses are magnificent—black and glossy with proud heads and high tails. They know it too; the silly creatures prance like they are from the king's personal stables.

But when they get closer, I realize the group's leader is familiar—he's the man I met in the streets of Stali.

Akello spots me shortly after I see him, and his eyes widen with surprise. "Lady Lucia?"

He swings down from his horse and nods to the rest

of the group. Recognizing him as well, Sebastian crosses his arms.

"I'd say fancy meeting you here and ask how you're doing, but from the general windblown, desert-beaten look of the lot of you, I think it's safe to assume you've been better," Akello says.

And though I don't want to, I admit, "Our mules and donkeys were stolen several nights ago."

He nods, looking genuinely concerned but not all that surprised. "I've heard bandits have been spotted in these parts. They robbed a caravan not two days from here."

I don't think we're dealing with common bandits, but I see no reason to voice my thoughts out loud. It's clear that someone is trying to keep us from the lily.

"Thankfully we stumbled on you," Akello continues. "We don't have extra horses, but Malka isn't far." He turns to his men. "Would any of you be willing to stay here for the night so our new friends can ride to the city?"

Sebastian doesn't look impressed with the "new friends" statement, but we are at their mercy, and he knows it.

Several men volunteer, and we break camp. My new temporary ride is far taller than my little donkey, and Avery has to give me a boost up.

"I see the captain has returned after all," Akello says, eying Avery.

"And we're married," I tell him sweetly, adding a tiny barb to my words.

He smiles knowingly. "Congratulations."

I eye him for half a moment and then nudge my horse forward.

"New friend?" Avery asks quietly as we ride side by side.

"I don't trust him." I keep my voice low, not wanting Akello or any of his men to overhear me.

Avery nods and drops the subject.

We arrive in Malka well after dark, but the city is alight.

"City of lanterns," Akello says to us as we reach the huge, stone bridge that crosses the wide, lazy river and leads us into a residential district.

Malka is true to its moniker. Decorative lanterns hang from every balcony, every signpost, every tree. There are simple lanterns and spherical works of art— lanterns of iron and copper and bronze. Fat, white pillar candles burn in every single one.

I openly gawk, unable to look away. Unlike the other cities we've seen in Elrija, Malka's buildings are primarily built of ivory stone, accented with massive, dark, wooden beams.

Boats with ridged fanlike sails glide along the river below us, and people call to each other from the nearby bank. Even at this late hour, the city is bustling. Some people head to the agricultural district just outside the city, and others linger, watching the water.

It takes several minutes to cross the bridge; the sleepy river is that wide. It will be a sight to see in the morning.

"The caravanserai is nearby," Akello says. "Or there are small inns and taverns scattered about the districts."

Sebastian nods. "The caravanserai will be fine."

We end up in front of a building that's easily as grand as the one we stayed in our first few nights in Elrija. Where Stali's caravanserai had the large, shallow pool, Malka has winding gardens, lit with even more lanterns. There's a bubbling fountain near the entrance, built to look like a waterfall. The effect is that of an oasis in the desert. Several caravans are set up at the edges, and even at this late hour, people are doing business.

"I suppose this is where we part ways," Akello says, after the attendants fetch our trunks and baggage.

"Thank you for your assistance," Sebastian says.

No matter how we got here, it's a relief to be back in civilization.

"You are most welcome. I will be in Malka for several weeks." He meets my eyes. "I'm sure we'll be seeing more of each other."

With that, Akello and the few men who joined him ride back into the streets, leading the extra horses with them. It's quite the sight, and people stop to gawk at the parade of midnight creatures. I watch them go, frowning. Akello was nothing but kind and helpful, but I cannot shake my first impression.

"Why the pensive face?" Avery asks.

I turn to the captain. "I've learned from experience that sometimes when people rescue you, they actually want to tag along and steal your orchids."

Avery gives me a wry smile. "You mean lily, I believe."

"It was odd he showed up, wasn't it?" I say, ignoring him.

Avery shrugs. "Honestly, Lucia. I have no idea. Sometimes, things are just a coincidence, and I for one am glad to be out of the desert."

I take a deep breath of the sweet flower-scented air and close my eyes. "I am as well."

"Do you know the very first thing I want to do once we get our rooms?" he asks, suggestively letting his finger wander down my arm.

I laugh. "Clean up?"

He grins. "You know me too well. I'm going straight to the bathhouse to soak for hours. If you're lucky, I'll be back before morning."

"Oh, you'll be back long before that."

The captain raises an eyebrow and steps closer. "Is that right?"

I give him a promising smile and hurry after the others.

16
SURELY NOT

The healer frowns with his hand hovering over my stomach. A faint bluish glow of magic radiates from his palm. After several moments, he nods and steps back.

"Well?" I demand.

We've been in Malka for two weeks now, trying to track down the city which seems to have never existed, and my stomach problems are getting worse. I've managed to keep it from Avery so far, but I know it's going to be an impossible task soon. I'm hoping that whatever this is, the physician can refer me to an apothecary, and I'll put all this behind me.

"You're very healthy," he says as he offers his hand, helping me rise to a sitting position on his table. "I'm going to refer you to a midwife I often work with. She can recommend a tincture for your nausea."

I stare at him for several long moments. "A midwife?"

"Yes, congratulations, Lucia. I believe you're about eight weeks pregnant."

A slightly horrified laugh bubbles up in my throat, but then my mind whirls madly with calculations. He must be wrong. "I'm sorry, but that can't be. I've only been married six, and I assure you nothing tawdry happened before the ceremony."

Not *that* tawdry anyway.

It's obvious the man is trying not to laugh. "It's all a matter of how we calculate cycles and—"

I hold up my hand. "Never mind. I believe you."

Feeling on the edge of hysteria, I take a long, deep breath and dig my fingers into the edge of the table. It had to have happened in Stali. How does a person fall pregnant the first night?

How?

I half listen as he gives me directions to the midwife's shoppe. After paying the woman at the front counter, I walk numbly through the streets. It's mid-afternoon, and the chatter of the huge flocks of seabirds on the river-bank can be heard all the way in the middle of the city. It's busy today, and the walkways are crowded.

Somehow, I manage to locate the midwife's shoppe and I stare at it for several moments before I abruptly turn on my heel and walk back to the caravanserai. Avery, Sebastian, and Gorin spoke of going to the library again this afternoon. If I'm lucky, Adeline will have stayed behind.

I knock on her door. When she doesn't answer in the next two seconds, I knock again...and again and again.

Finally, her door flies open, and she stands on the other side, looking flustered. "Lucia! For goodness sake —what's the matter with you?"

I push her into the room and pull the door shut. As an afterthought, I lock it for good measure and then finally turn around.

"What happened?" Then, remembering where I told her I was sneaking off to this morning, she demands, "What did the doctor say? Are you all right?"

"No."

Her eyes widen with concern. "Lucia—"

"He said I'm pregnant!"

She flinches at the direct term, but then she purses her lips, trying not to smile.

"Adeline!"

"It's just that..." She starts to laugh, unable to stop herself. "I thought you had come down with some wasting disease from the look on your face."

I glare at her.

Realizing that I'm as rattled as I am, she sighs. "How far along are you?"

"Eight weeks."

"And you didn't *notice?*" she asks, incredulous.

"I've been a little busy, tracking down maps and facing wraiths and getting stranded in the desert," I hiss.

She sighs, sympathetic, but there's something about the look in her eyes...

I suck in a sharp breath and point an accusing finger at her. "You're giddy about this! You're already planning tiny wardrobes and bonnets and..."

Pressing a hand to my stomach, I sit, feeling ill.

I am not nearly mature enough to have a baby. I can barely take care of Flink. What if it grows up the same way? What if my mothering skills are so below par, that everything I raise ends up being a wretched, unruly beast?

"I believe it's normal that you're a little disconcerted," Adeline says in her best, soothing voice, "but once you tell the captain, you'll begin to feel better."

"Do I have to?"

Adeline sits across from me, looking baffled. "Have to what?"

"Tell Avery?"

She raises a perfect brow. "Even if you don't, he's going to figure it out soon enough."

And suddenly, the unbidden image of me waddling through the desert like a bloated cow, running from a mess of cobras, leaps into my mind.

"Adeline, how am I going to finish the expedition?" I ask, snapping out of my melodramatic fit. Completely serious, I sit up. "I can't go running into wraiths like this."

She nibbles her lip, thinking. "I'm sure Avery would take you back to Kalae. The rest of us can stay and look for the lily."

"No." I shake my head, determined. "I've never abandoned a job, and I owe this to Gorin. Besides, my mother was constantly pregnant while I was young, and she managed it."

"Running a farm might be slightly different than exploring ruins..."

"I'm fine." In this moment, I make up my mind. I am fine. I *will* be fine. Perhaps this expedition isn't going exactly according to plan, but we've gotten past cobras and scorpions and life-sucking specters. I'm not going to let a little thing like a tiny human thwart it.

"ARE YOU ALL RIGHT?" Avery asks, studying my plate.

"I'm *fine*."

And I am. I know because I tell myself repeatedly, several dozen times a day.

His eyebrows shoot up, and he sits back. Then that irritatingly perfect smirk spreads across his face. "Are you sure about that? Because you aren't eating—still."

I need to ask the midwife about that, but I haven't worked up the nerve to visit her. My appetite is gone, and half the things I used to love—meat, coffee, fish—smell awful. And eggs? Just the thought makes me green around the edges.

"I ate," I argue.

And I did—three bites of grouse and a roll. Half the problem is the spices. The very thing that made Elrijan food smell so delicious when we first arrived is what's causing my stomach to churn now.

"This has been going on for weeks." He's smiling, but he looks concerned. "Don't you think it's time you see a physician?"

We're in a small tavern off the river, sitting on a balcony that overlooks the water. We're alone, which has been the nicest thing about staying in Malka. As a group, we scour for information on the village with the dragon bridge during the day and then go about our own business at night. Avery and I have had plenty of time alone, and it's beginning to feel like we're doing more than pretending we're married.

It's also given me plenty of time to tell him about the baby situation. And yet, I haven't.

I set my napkin over my plate, letting the fabric block the offensive smells that insist on wafting in my general direction. "Avery, I need to speak with you."

Perhaps sensing the dread in my expression, the captain abandons the rest of his dinner and lays his arms on the table, waiting for me to begin. He has an anxious look about him, as if he's waiting for bad news.

I look at the table. "I saw a physician a week ago."

"When?"

"That doesn't matter." I wave the question away. "But he told me—"

"It was the wraith, wasn't it?" he breathes, leaning forward, his eyes intense with worry. "I knew something—"

Unable to keep him in misery, I clench my eyes shut and cut him off, "We're going to have a baby."

His silence is so loud, I peek my eyes open slowly, worried he might have passed out. I find him staring at me, a half-smile on his lips, his eyes narrowed. "Lucia? Are you serious?"

I nod, almost ashamed, like I've done something wrong even though he certainly played his part. "It must have happened in Stali."

His smile is growing. "You don't suppose it was our first night?"

"If not, it must have been close to it."

I narrow my eyes as he leans forward with an expression that's beginning to irk me. He gives me a wicked grin, raising his eyebrows, looking...something. It takes me several moments, but then I realize what it is—he's *proud* of himself.

Groaning, I toss my napkin at him.

His smile falls. "You're not happy?"

"Happy? I'm terrified!"

With a carefree expression that makes me envious, he tosses several coins on the table and offers me his hand. "It's a nice evening. Let's go for a walk."

I accept his arm, and we amble along the streets. There are several benches on the bridge that look out over the water, and Avery stops at the first one available.

"How are you so calm about all this?" I demand as soon as we sit.

An egret wades near the bank, his long legs in the water. I watch him for several moments before turning back to Avery.

"I'm as nervous as you are." He takes my hand and winds his fingers with mine. "But I know it's going to be all right—better than all right. Perfect."

"You realize I can't even bring up a dragon properly, don't you?"

He grins, shaking his head. "Lucia, a baby is not a dragon. And you're forgetting something significant."

"What?"

Avery leans close and sets his hand on my shoulder. "You're not doing this alone. We're in this together—we're a family now."

"I can't even boil water. How can I be a mother if I can't *cook?*"

He gives me the strangest look. "Lucia, I thought I made this clear. We have a fair amount of money to our name. You don't need to cook—ever."

That makes me take pause. "Ever?"

"Not unless you want to."

"I won't." I pin him with my eyes, making sure he understands.

He grins. "Understood."

I finally give into his good mood. I settle my back against the bench and look out at the water, taking our clasped hands and setting them in my lap. There's one more question I need to ask him. "Tell me the truth—were you a terror as a child?"

Avery nods, serious. "The worst."

17
DRAGON BRIDGE

Malka's library is dark and rather depressing —not the best place to spend every spare minute of the last several weeks. Gorin is beside himself. None of the scholars have heard of the dragon bridge; no one knows what Elrijan village was sieged by Kalaens in these modern times. We're nearing the end of the month, and we have less than thirty days to find the lily.

My nose itches as I slap another dusty book closed. As I rub it, I scowl at the towering stack next to me. Though dark, the library is extensive, and their geography section is quite impressive. Of course, that just means we have more books to sort through.

I've deviated from our original task and started looking up legends and stories instead, hoping to find lore on the healing spring or the lily that grows there. I've learned several interesting facts, even if nothing hinted at the location of either.

First, the water is far more potent than the lily, but it loses its power if it's transported from the spring. That's why the flower is so valuable—it holds its healing properties long after it's picked. Some of those properties are retained even after the flower is dried, though ancient alchemists tried to make their concoctions before that point.

Second, several of the texts hint at side effects, but nothing goes into detail.

However, none of this knowledge will do us any good if we can't locate the wretched things.

Avery comes up behind me, brushes my hair aside, and grazes his lips over the back of my neck. "Find anything?" he murmurs.

"Dust."

"How are you feeling?"

"Better."

Avery dragged me to the midwife the day after I gave him the news. The tea the woman gave me helps, though I'm still exhausted. She assured me that would pass. Apparently, there is a small window of time—after all this nausea and before I look like a whale—that I will feel quite good. I wish it would hurry up.

"Set those aside." Avery sets his hands on my shoulders and kneads my tense muscles, making me melt. "Let's get some air."

I glance at Gorin, who's a few tables away. The poor man sits slumped over, his hands in his hair, staring at the book in front of him. For as many as he has set in the discard pile, there are two more to read. I'm not even sure he slept last night. He looks awful.

"I shouldn't," I say with a sigh, opening another book.

Still behind me, Avery rests his chin on my head. He points to an illustration on the page in front of me. "I've seen those before."

It's a yellow flower, similar to a buttercup.

"*Yilentalis cruipitum,*" I read carefully.

Yancey walks up to our table and frowns at Avery. "Dragon weed."

The captain stands so slowly, I angle in the chair to face him. He rubs his chin, thinking. "Is that what it's called?"

Our alchemist shrugs. "It's what we call it in Kalae."

Avery wears the strangest expression. I touch his arm. "What is it?"

A slow smile stretches across his lips, and his eyes light as if something just clicked into place. He grabs me by the hand and pulls me to my feet. "Come with me."

"Where are we going?"

"Out." I start to laugh as he hurries me along. Over his shoulder, he calls, "Gorin! I've got it!"

This, of course, earns him several nasty looks from the scholarly types who have been kind enough to let us study in their guild library.

"Listen here, young man—" an elderly woman starts.

He catches her hand and bows his head to her, grinning as he drops his voice to an acceptable level. "My sincerest apologies, madam."

She flushes, probably unused to such attention. "I suppose it's all right—but be quiet from now on."

"Of course," he promises, and then he tugs me through the aisles and out the door.

By the time we reach the street, we're almost running.

"Avery!" I gasp, laughing, more surprised than out of breath. "Are we in that much of a hurry?"

He stops so abruptly, we end up causing a block in the street traffic. Several people mutter about mindless Kalaens as they walk around us.

"Are you all right?" he asks, instantly concerned. His eyes search my face.

We're still adjusting to the news, and Avery's dealt with it by treating me as if I'm made of glass.

"I'm fine."

"But you say that every time."

"That's because I'm *fine* most of the time. If you didn't ask me every five seconds, you might receive a more colorful variety of answers."

He raises an eyebrow. "You're crabby. Do you need to eat something?"

That's another thing the midwife informed us of—I'll feel better if I eat several small meals all through the day. Now Avery's continually trying to shove food down my throat.

I grit my teeth before I answer. "I love you, you know that, right?"

Looking handsome even when he's baffled, he nods.

I continue, "Then don't take this the wrong way

when I say this, but if you try to feed me one more time, I'm going to stab you."

Wisely biting back a smile, he nods. "Noted."

"I mean it."

"And I believe you."

Before the conversation can go any further, Gorin and the rest of our group join us. We follow Avery through the streets at a slightly saner pace until we reach the district around the artist's guild. Unlike most cities, especially those in Kalae, Malka's artists' guild is far larger than the one belonging to their mages. Several murals decorate the stone walls. They're beautiful, intricate works of art, most depicting desert landscapes.

"Look," Avery says, holding his hands up in front of one of them.

Hundreds of yellow flowers vine over a sandstone arch. There are mountains depicted in the distance, tall ones with jagged, white peaks.

"It's a bridge...of dragon weed," I say slowly. "You don't think this is our—

"Dragon bridge," Gorin whispers.

"Those are the Castleridge mountains," Yancey says.

I turn, surprised he bothered to join us. Esme stands by his side, frowning. "Where's Castleridge?"

"Maywell," Sebastian says. "In the provinces, far to the northwest."

Gorin shakes his head. "Why would an Elrijan artist depict a Kalaen landscape on a wall in Malka?"

Understanding dawns on me, fast and sure. "Because the land didn't always belong to Kalae."

"ARE YOU LEAVING MALKA?" Akello asks as we saddle the new horses Avery, Sebastian, and Gorin pitched in to buy. They aren't as grand as the black steeds we rode into the city, but they are fine enough for our trip over the border. At least I don't have to ride a donkey this time.

I glance at Akello. The man's been around the city this last month, and he checks in on us occasionally. Though he's done nothing wrong, I can't shake the strange feeling I have about him. He just has the air of a shifty person, though, for the life of me, I can't place why.

"We are headed to Kalae," I tell him.

He gives me a knowing nod. "It is difficult, but sometimes it's best to cut our losses when we've set our sights on the unattainable."

"And just what were our sights set on?" I ask, cocking my head.

"Gorin told me you're after the legendary lily that grows in the healing spring." He smiles. "But, adventuress, I assure you, the spring and the lily are both myths."

Because he looks so high and mighty now that he thinks we're giving up, I almost tell him we're not yet done searching for the lily. Just before I do, I stop myself. Let him think we're going home.

Unfortunately, Gorin comes up behind me. "Actually, I think we're finally on the right track. From our research, we believe the spring's location is marked on a pillar in a ruin just outside Elrija."

Akello raises his eyebrows at me, amusement tugging at his lips. "Is that so?"

I turn back to my horse. "We'll see."

"You must be careful. I've heard the bandits are getting braver, prowling during the day."

"We'll keep our eyes open."

"I could come with you, offer you protection. For a price, of course."

But who would protect us from Akello?

"That won't be nece—" I begin just to have Gorin cut me off.

"We would be much obliged."

I turn back to the two, not liking this one bit. "I'm sure Akello has better things to do than traipse through the desert with us."

The man meets my eyes. "On the contrary, this is exactly what I do."

"Do?"

"I'm a mercenary, Lucia. I work where the money is —protect those who need protecting."

"You make it sound like a noble profession."

Akello bows, already walking away to make arrangements. "Take my word for it—it can be quite noble indeed."

I glare at Gorin as soon as the man's gone. "Why did you agree?"

Gorin looks surprised. "He saved us in the desert,

Lucia. And with all the strange things we've had happen, it cannot hurt to have a hired blade with us."

That might be true—if it were anyone other than Akello.

18
LOOK AT THE LOVELY WEBS

The trip to the northern border takes six and a half uneventful days. We don't find any dead crows around our campfires; we are not gifted with cobras. The trip is almost too peaceful, and I am on edge because of it.

Also, now that I have past my second month, riding is less comfortable, and it wasn't pleasant before—especially on a donkey.

"How are you feel—" Avery stops when I flash him a look of death, and he grins. "You know, I rather like you like this, all spunk and sass."

I narrow my eyes at him.

He rides closer and leans toward me so only I will hear him. "Perhaps we should have a dozen children?"

Staring right at him, I set my hand on the hilt of my new dagger. As he always does when we have this exchange, he laughs.

Though I haven't spoken a word of my *condition*, the

news has spread. Sebastian sends me wary looks, acting almost as concerned for my wellbeing as Avery but far more horrified. Adeline, bless her sweet, obnoxious self, has already started stitching a tiny blanket. The rest couldn't care less, and Yancey blatantly avoids the subject.

We follow a road that hasn't been traveled for what looks like ages, and we've entered a valley that could almost—almost—be considered a meadow. The ground here is clay, and our path was rutted by carts traveling through after a heavy rain. Weeds and grass took over long ago, and it's difficult to find our way.

There are no cities, no villages, and we don't pass a soul on our travels. It's a road forgotten, and we don't even find a border guard. By far, this has been the easiest leg of our journey. Call me cynical, but that makes me wonder what terrible mishap is waiting for us once we reach Maywell.

We must be on the right road because right ahead of us looms a stone arch the size of a building. It's a magnificent sight, naturally carved directly from the mountain. Even early in the season, vines climb over it, just like in the mural. There are no flowers yet, but the Castleridge mountains rise on the other side, sentinels in the distance. Seeing them and their green and blue hillsides makes me long for my home kingdom.

I'm so tired of the desert.

Gorin leads us under the arch, and we get our first glimpse of the ruins. It's a village carved right into the cliff face, under the protection of an overhanging rock ledge. It's older than Struin Aria and far smaller. Not more than ten families could have lived here, perhaps a few more. Most of the clay and stone houses show their neglect. Roofs are caved in; entire walls crumbled long ago. The small buildings all seem connected by stairs and walkways, but those too are in a sad state.

I look at Avery, curious what his reaction will be. Just as I expect, he looks like a young child, eager to explore.

"No robbing tombs," I tell him.

He flashes me a broad, not-so-innocent grin. "I would never."

Sebastian slows his horse to walk next to us. "Look there, right in the center of the village."

A pillar—*the* pillar.

"Do you think that's it?" I ask. "It almost seems too easy."

"After all we've been through, it's time for something to go well."

No argument there.

Gorin dismounts just before the ruin, which seems wise. When the village was at it's prime, I am almost certain the stables were below. The pathways look as if they were built for foot traffic only.

Flink wanders away as soon as we stop, off to explore. He's happy to be out of the city, where he was forced to spend most of his time in our room in the cara-vanserai. We saw little of him on the way here, but he always returned in the evening, checking in, scrounging for food.

Yancey gets off his horse and walks to Esme, ready to

offer her a hand. Akello beats him to it. The alchemist narrows his eyes, and turns away, looking slightly irked.

Esme gives Akello a tight smile. I've watched her around him, and though I haven't spoken with her, I believe she trusts him as little as I do.

"I'm not sure the ruin is stable," Avery says, running a sharp eye over the tiny village. "Perhaps you should wait here."

I give him a withering look and lead the way up the ruins.

"Lucia—" my oh-so-protective husband continues.

Whipping around, I give him a look that makes most people back off. It's never worked on him.

In answer, he holds up his hands, laughing. "Just be careful, all right?"

I roll my eyes, but I can't help but smile. He's going to drive me mad. How in the world am I going to survive seven more months of this?

"Lucia, we have a problem," Sebastian calls from ahead of me. Because Avery slowed me down, he beat me to the pillar. I jog the rest of the way, and he motions to the cylindrical stone. "There's nothing here."

Frowning, I examine the surface for signs of extreme erosion. And, yes, time and weather have taken their toll, but not so much as to wipe out an entire etching.

Akello leans on a low wall just outside the ruin, watching but not participating. Apparently mercenaries are only handy in a skirmish. Even Yancey is making himself useful—sort of. He's walking about, frowning as if he's deep in thought when in truth, he's probably wondering what and when we're going to eat.

The alchemist pokes at something with his foot. "There's another level below."

He then leans down and shoves a heavy stone disk along the ground. It makes a horrible noise, and the entire ruin trembles. I glance around, not entirely sure it won't come crashing down around us.

Esme joins Yancey and gives the newly-uncovered hole an uncertain look. "You know, the last time we went down one of these, we found a nest of wraiths."

Sebastian brushes dirt and dry, crumbling leaves away from the base of the pillar. He looks up at me, resigned. "I believe the pillar goes down."

"So the map might be below?" I ask.

"I think there's a good chance."

Adeline casts her light spell and gives Sebastian a smile that's forced but trying to be eager. "I'm ready."

Sebastian gives her a questioning look. "Are you sure?"

She nods, attempting to be brave.

"I'm not going down there," Esme says, crossing her arms.

Yancey looks at her, a rotten expression on his face. "Scared?"

Oddly, she glances at Akello, and I can't help but wonder if she's worried he's going to trap us as soon as we're down. The mercenary looks back, his face expressionless and his dark eyes unreadable.

I'm just about to go down the dusty stairs Yancey

uncovered when Avery gently takes my arm. "You're not going to like me for saying this, but I think it would be best if you were to stay up here with Esme."

"Avery!" I hiss quietly, exasperated. "You cannot continue to coddle me like this."

"I'm not, I just..." he glances down.

There are very few times I've seen the captain uncertain, and it stirs something in my heart. It's not enough to make me loiter about while they do the work, but still. It's sweet in its own frustrating way.

"Fine," he says with a sigh, smart enough to realize he's not going to win this argument. "Seeing as you have your bow this time."

I walk down the steps, hesitant. Slowly, my eyes adjust to Adeline's dim light. We're in a small room, an octagonal chamber with eight doorways. Spiderwebs decorate the space like satin tassels in a royal carriage. My skin is already crawling.

"Remind you of our friend from the island?" Avery whispers in my ear, bringing up the goat-sized tarantula.

It's nice to see some things have gone back to normal.

Just as I'm spinning, taking in the place, Adeline's light flickers. I whirl around to face her, knowing that's a bad sign. Her eyes are glued to something on the floor, and as soon as I follow her gaze, I wish I hadn't.

"Skeleton in the corner," Avery says, less than amused. "And my darling wife wants to explore."

"That's...a..." Adeline gulps as her light stutters. "I mean, was that...human?"

No one answers her, but Gorin wrinkles his nose at the bones and decomposing...matter. Even Yancey looks unsettled.

Avery, *being Avery*, kneels next to the skeleton and then looks at us over his shoulder. "He has a rather terrified look about him, don't you think? What with him being in the fetal position with his arms covering his face and all."

"Not helping," Sebastian hisses under his breath.

The captain shrugs. "Wouldn't it be prudent of us to question how the fellow died?"

Gorin points to a dagger under the bones. "That might have something to do with it."

Avery notices the dagger for the first time, and he grins. Without the slightest hesitation, he reaches under the ribcage, through thick spiderwebs, and plucks the blade from the ground, receiving a chorus of quiet groans from the rest of us. He holds it up, examining it. "Too bad it's not enchanted. Still—look at those rubies." He whistles, awfully proud of his find.

"What did we talk about?" I ask, mostly teasing. "Respectable captains do not rob tombs."

My husband rises to his feet, stalking toward me. "Who said anything about respectable? I thought I was a pirate?"

"And I thought that nonsense would stop after you got married," Sebastian says, looking unsettled. Before Avery can retort, he looks around. "What doorway do we try first?"

I point to the one to our immediate left. "I believe that one's closest to the pillar."

Adeline cranes her neck to look at the archway as we pass, her eyes trained on the thick and silky webs. "Where are the spiders do you think?"

She doesn't sound like she truly wants to know.

Again, Avery walks behind me and leans close to my ear. "Waiting for fresh blood." Then he tickles my sides with a featherlight, tiny-arachnid-feet touch, making my skin crawl. I lightly elbow him in the stomach, and he laughs in my ear.

Bless the tiny village. As soon as we're in the room, we find the pillar. It stands at the very center, just as Sebastian predicted. There are old tables here, covered in ages of dust. They stand intact, safe from the weather and sun.

"It was an alchemy chamber," Yancey says as he studies the room.

"How can you tell?" Adeline asks.

He points to a dozen mortars, pestles, shears, and earthen jars, turning to look at her as if she's daft. But her eyes still linger on the webs above us.

I couldn't care less about the room; my eyes are glued to the pillar. "It's a map!" I say excitedly as I kneel in front of it.

Gorin's right behind me, even more eager than I. He scans it with his finger, murmuring names of landmarks and cities to himself. Finally, his finger comes to rest on a spot far to the south of Elrija, near the sea. "Here!"

Elated, as a group, we let out a quiet, collective cry of

jubilation. Well, Adeline's might be of the please-let-this-be-over-as-soon-as-possible variety, and Yancey's is an are-we-finished-yet sort of groan of relief.

Sebastian's already pulling a rolled piece of parchment and charcoal from his pack, ready to do the etching. Kneeling feels strange, like my stomach is oddly heavy even though I'm not yet showing, and I stand to make room for Sebastian. I wander the room, taking in the engraved art on the walls. I poke about the alchemy supplies, curious what might be lying around.

One jar contains salt and another crystallized honey. I open a third pot, curious. But it's not an ingredient— it's a nest of silk webs. Startled, I gasp and drop the brittle jar. It breaks on the table and suddenly, hundreds of tiny red spiders emerge from the cocoon. I stumble back, letting out a piercing shriek that echoes through the entire underground chamber.

The tiniest bit of dust falls from the ceiling, and I back away from the table. "Hurry, Sebastian!"

"What did you do?" he demands, half-finished with the rubbing. "Lucia—"

"What's that?" Adeline demands.

We all fall silent. I hear it too—it sounds like millions and millions of tiny scampering, crawling...

Adeline screams first. Scarlet, coin-sized spiders erupt from every nook and cubby, crawling out of holes and crevices and seams in the rock. Spiders *everywhere.*

"Leave it, Sebastian!" I scream as we leap for the exit.

In her terror, Adeline's already halfway out, leaving us in partial darkness. Avery shoves me ahead, pushing me to the exit. Feeling as if half a dozen of the spiders are on me, I run as fast as I can. Even when I burst into the sunlight, the sensation of their imaginary feet crawling over me makes me shudder uncontrollably. Adeline's dusting herself off at a frantic rate, and I do the same. The men burst out of the chamber right behind us, and Yancey shoves the stone disk back into place.

"What happened?" Esme demands, her eyes wide with worry as we flail.

After several long moments, much to our relief, we realize we don't have any stowaways. Suddenly, Gorin goes completely still. "Lucia," he whispers, horrified. "Don't move. There's a crimson assassin on your arm. If it bites you, there's no antidote."

I freeze as well, my mind skittering with horror.

Avery tries to rush to me, but Sebastian holds him back. "No, Yancey's closer—and calmer."

The alchemist walks to me slowly, his gaze on my shoulder and his hands steady. "I'm going to whisk it away."

"Mmmm," I manage. From the corner of my eye, I see the spider moving up my arm, and I can now feel it on my bare skin.

I hate the desert. I hate its cobras and scorpions and wraiths, and I really, truly *loathe* its spiders.

Yancey raises his hand, preparing his air manipulation spell, but then he stops.

"Yancey," I plead, not daring to move. "Just get it over with."

"If it goes the wrong direction, it could bite you."

Only now does he sound nervous, and that terrifies me. "I'll have to flick it off with my hand."

"Be careful," Esme pleads.

Adeline's tucked into Sebastian's arms with her face buried against his chest, unable to watch. I can barely breathe. Only one thought runs through my mind, over and over and over: If I die, then the baby dies with me. Would it feel pain? Would it hurt?

The thought is horrifying, but I cannot give in to the slightest sob. If I do, if I tremble at all, that might be all it takes for the spider to feel threatened.

Yancey steps right in front of me, bending his knees so he's at my eye level. "I've got this, do you understand? I won't let it bite you, but you must not move a muscle."

I close my eyes, preparing myself.

Then I feel it, the quick flick of Yancey's hand on my shoulder. Around us, our companions gasp, and my eyes fly open. As if time has slowed, instead of falling to the ground, the spider sends out a web, and the thin string carries it right to Yancey. The alchemist leaps back, trying to avoid it, but it's too late. It lands on his arm.

Not even a full second later, he knocks the crimson assassin to the ground and smashes it under his boot. My relief is so intense, I double over. After a moment, I look back up. Yancey's still staring at the ground.

"Are you all right?" I ask.

He meets my eyes, his face unusually pale, and he holds out his arm. A tiny red welt already forms just below his elbow.

19
JUST A TINY BITE

Horrified, I stare at the wound. "Yancey!"

He lowers his arm, almost looking as if he plans to ignore the bite. "It's not that bad."

Esme, getting the drift of the conversation, is on him in an instant. She pulls his arm up, ignoring his protests, and her face goes white. "*No*," she whispers.

I turn to Gorin. "You said there's no antidote."

Our guide looks ashen. "There isn't."

"What about something to slow the poison," I demand. "*Anything.*"

"I have charcoal," Yancey says from behind me. "I'll make a paste and see if I can draw it out."

I turn and study him. At first glance, he looks unconcerned, but the truth is, he's dying right in front of us. He hides his worry well, but it's there in the lines at the edges of his eyes, in the way he presses his lips together.

"I'll do it," Esme says, grasping his hand. "Tell me what to do—tell me what to make, and I'll do it."

He looks at her for several long seconds. Something passes between them, something heartbreaking. "All right."

Together, they go to his horse, off to sort through his pack.

Sebastian steps close to Gorin, but his eyes are on Yancey. "There must be something we can do for him. We can't just watch him die."

"The spring," I say suddenly, hope washing over me like warm sunshine. I grab Avery. "It will heal him, won't it?"

Gorin's eyes widen at the thought. He nods slowly at first, but the motion becomes more sure. "Yes, it will. But we only have ten days before the poison finishes its work, and" —he takes the just-finished rubbing right from Sebastian's hand, frowning— "it will take at least twelve days to travel there."

I watch Esme earnestly make the paste just as Yancey directs. Her focus is solely on her task, and she wears a look of sheer determination. But Yancey's eyes are on the tall, pretty Elrijan woman—on her hair, on her face. He looks like he's taking her in, committing her to memory. It's a wistful look, perfectly devastating.

Choking back the emotion tightening my throat, I turn to the men. "We will make it. We have no choice."

They nod in agreement, and we part, already mounting our horses.

"Hurry it up, Yancey," I call, trying to sound light and confident. "We have to get you to the spring."

Esme stares at me blankly, and then she understands. She sets a hand over her mouth, and her shoulders shake as she turns away from the group, overcome with relief.

Yancey, who must have come to terms with his fate in this short period of time, stars at me dumbly.

I lean forward in my saddle, making him meet my eyes. "The spring will heal you, Yancey, but you have to get your massive self on your horse right this moment, or we'll never make it in time."

He blinks at me, and then he nods.

Done crying, with tear trails running down her face, Esme turns, shoves all the supplies back in Yancey's pack, and yanks him to his horse. Once they're ready, we turn our horses back toward the dragon bridge arch. I pass Akello.

The mercenary has stayed silent this whole time, but his eyes meet mine now. Quietly, he says, "You should have gone home. The desert isn't safe."

I glance at Yancey, and guilt writhes in my stomach.

"It's not too late to go back to Kalae. I would hate for something to happen to you, Lucia." Though the words are chilling, and frankly, a little ominous, his expression is sincere.

"It's too late now," I answer quietly. "If there's even the slightest chance we can save Yancey, we're going to take it."

The man nods, obviously expecting nothing less.

～

I COUNT THE DAYS, and each seems to go faster than the last. Time is against us, and it's slipping through our fingers. The desert is brutal. With every spring day we lose, we creep closer to summer, and the sun grows more unforgiving.

Esme rides next to Yancey, concern etched in her expression. She keeps a watchful eye on the alchemist, making sure he doesn't topple right off his horse. I'm not sure what she would do about it if he did.

We ride fast, traveling day and night, stopping only to rest a few hours at a time during the hottest part of the afternoon. By the fifth day, we're all dead on our horses, and Yancey's failing fast. A blue bruise spreads around the wound, a sure sign the tissue is dying.

Today, he began to sweat, and he clears his throat often, as if there is an obstruction.

"He can't go on like this," I overhear Adeline say to Sebastian as we ride.

My business partner nods, but there is nothing we can do. We press on because we have no alternative. Each day, Avery grows more concerned, but it's not Yancey who has his attention. He watches me, looking for signs of extreme exhaustion, for signs that I've pushed myself too hard.

And I do ache, though I've told no one. Every once in a while, I wince from a sharp pain, but I hide my discomfort as best I can for Yancey's sake.

"Let's stop for a few hours," Gorin calls when we reach a copse of large boulders that cast a little shade.

The sun is high in the sky, and the heat is sweltering. I stay in my saddle, too tired to move, wanting nothing more than a bath and a soft bed. At the very least, a cool breeze. I'd even settle for a *lukewarm* breeze at this point —anything but the sporadic, bone-dry gusts that kick up sand and debris.

"Avery," I say, still atop my horse. If my stomach didn't feel so heavy and awkward, I'd lie against my horse's neck. I'm barely showing, but it feels as if I swallowed lead.

My husband is at my side in an instant. His eyes take me in, and he frowns. "I'd ask if you're doing all right, but I've been forbidden from uttering those words."

I give him a tired smile. "Help me down."

Instantly, his hands are on my waist, and he gently assists me from my horse. Exhausted, I rest against him. I could fall asleep right here. Quietly, so no one will hear me, I say, "I want to go home, Avery."

He wraps his arms around my back. "Is that a request?"

I think about it for a moment. He'd take me away right now if I wanted him to. Sebastian wouldn't mind; neither would Adeline. Gorin might panic a bit, but Sebastian is every bit as capable as I am.

Let's be honest: Sebastian is every bit *more* capable than I am.

We could go home, just Avery and me. We could

sleep in a real bed tonight and not get up until noon the next day.

After several moments of selfish indecision, I shake my head.

Because we don't stop long, we don't bother with the tents anymore. We toss out the bedrolls and collapse on top of them. I fall asleep as soon as I stretch out on the hard, prickly ground. It seems, however, that as soon as I close my eyes, it's time to get up.

Avery's still asleep beside me, so I linger a few minutes more. We've already overslept. The sun is low in the sky. We should have been up hours ago.

As I lie here, I idly listen to Esme as she speaks with Gorin.

No, not Gorin. Akello.

"I have done everything you've asked of me," she says quietly, sounding frantic. "You swore that if I helped you..."

My ears perk up, intent now on the conversation.

"What do you want from me? I have a job to do, Esme. It is unwise to double-cross..." Akello lowers his voice, and I cannot make out the last of his words.

They shift a little farther away, and now I can't hear them at all.

I turn back toward Avery, groaning as a rock stabs me in the back. When I turn to face the captain, his eyes are already open and alert.

"You heard that too?" I barely whisper.

"I did."

"What do you make of it?"

Avery shakes his head. "I don't know, but I don't like it."

"Should we confront them about it?"

"Not yet. But we'll be watchful."

Behind us, Sebastian rises. We too get up, acting as if we just woke. Esme comes back to camp and kneels by Yancey's side. Her eyes flicker over his pale face, and she bites her bottom lip.

"Yancey," she whispers as she sets a hand on his shoulder.

He groans in his sleep, but it's a weak sound.

"We have to go," she tells him softly as she rubs his arm, being careful to avoid the spreading wound.

I watch her, wondering what she could have possibly been talking to Akello about. Whatever it was, they didn't want the rest of us to hear.

What did Akello mean he has a job to do? Though it makes me feel unloyal to think it, I can't help but wonder if Esme has a reason to keep us from the spring. After all, most of the trouble started when she showed up at Struin Aria.

But when she looks at Yancey like that, I can't help but think that she's as desperate to find the spring as we are.

After a few long minutes, Yancey manages to pull himself to his feet with the men's assistance. He looks like death.

I don't know if he has five more days in him—I don't know if we'll find the spring by then even if he does. Esme follows him to his horse, wringing her hands as the men hoist him up. Her eyes meet mine, and she gives me a weak smile. Her expression flickers when I purse my lips and turn to my own horse.

We ride into the night and morning, taking brief breaks to keep Yancey hydrated. He quit eating a day ago.

Flink finds us, and he wanders about, looking at us all with his serious amber eyes, probably wondering why we're all so somber.

After each short break, we get on our horses and do it all over again.

Day six passes, and then day seven. I'm sick with exhaustion, and I begin to wonder if Avery's right. This can't be good for the baby. But what choice do we have?

On the beginning of day eight, my stomach cramps. The pain is so intense, I cry out and grasp hold of the reins to keep from falling.

Avery yanks his horse to mine and pulls me to a stop. I double over, waiting for the pain to subside.

"What is it?" Avery demands. His eyebrows are drawn low, and his eyes search mine, looking for the truth this time.

"It hurts," I finally admit.

He offers his hand, and from the look on his face, I know I'm going to have to acknowledge I'm not doing well.

"What hurts?" he whispers once my feet are on the ground.

I set my hand on my lower abdomen.

"Lucia," Avery says, taking me by the shoulders. "You can't keep going at this pace."

"Primtea," Yancey says, his voice barely above a scratchy whisper.

We all whip toward him, shocked. I thought he was out cold.

"In my pack." The alchemist shifts, but Esme's off her horse and at his side in less than a heartbeat.

She sets her hand on his arm. "Be still. I'll find it."

Esme rummages around for several moments and then pulls out a folded parchment. "This?"

Yancey gives her a single nod and draws in a deep breath. "Drink the tea, Lucia. Go back to Kalae."

Sebastian watches the exchange from atop his horse, and finally, he meets my eyes. Slowly, knowing it will kill me, he nods. "He's right. Lucia, you need go home."

"But Yancey," I protest even as another cramp paralyzes me. I grasp hold of Avery's arm, almost crying out.

Something's wrong. I feel it; I know it.

"We'll find the spring," Sebastian says. He turns his eyes on Yancey. "I swear."

Once the pain passes, I go to Yancey's side, standing in front of him so he can see me without turning his head. Lowering my voice so the others don't hear, I say, "I'm so sorry. This is my fault."

"You saved me from the siren; I saved you from the spider. We're even, adventuress."

He sounds so weak. I grasp his good arm as tears prick my eyes. "You will hold on until you reach the spring, do you understand me?"

It's not a request.

He chuckles, but it quickly morphs into a breathy

179

groan. "And you will take care of yourself and your baby."

I nod, and the tears finally escape. Another pain looms, and I squeeze his arm one more time before stepping away.

"Go," I say to Sebastian, not quite able to look at him.

Adeline's cheeks are wet, and she holds out her hand to me in a goodbye. Esme nods, and so does Gorin. Akello watches the ground, perhaps feeling as if he's intruded on something intensely personal.

And then they go, leaving Avery and me. Flink appears from behind a hill, hurrying after the group until he realizes that I've stayed. He ambles over to me and leans against my side, letting me pet his smooth scales.

Avery struggles to start a fire, preparing to boil water for the tea.

I toss our bedroll on the ground and lie down, desperate for rest. Too late, I realize we never warned Sebastian about Esme and Akello.

20
WHAT'S HER ELEMENT?

I lie in Avery's arms, safe against his chest, listening to the late morning sounds of the desert. A sand wren calls from her cliffside home, trilling a sweet song that carries on the breeze.

Because we knew we'd be sleeping more than two hours, Avery set up the tent last night. I slept like the dead, and I feel rejuvenated.

As we linger here together, enjoying the fact that we have nowhere to go and no time to be there, Avery idly runs his finger along my arm. The sensation is delicious, and it makes me want to close my eyes and go back to sleep.

"You know I'm going to ask you," he murmurs next to my temple.

I smile. "I don't hurt anymore."

He lets out a relieved breath. "And everything's...normal?"

"I think so." I roll onto my back, resting my head on his arm, still tucked close to him.

He touches me like I'm breakable, which after yesterday, I start to worry that maybe I am. With great care, he folds my loose bodice up a few inches and sets his palm on my stomach.

I squirm at first, self-conscious of my growing belly. It's not much, just a slight bump. But still.

Oblivious to my discomfort, Avery brushes his hand over my navel and turns to me. "Do you have any idea how worried I've been about you the last few days?"

"Avery," I say softly, melting the slightest bit. I look away, unable to keep my eyes locked on his liquid brown gaze. "I'm sorry."

His hand strays from my stomach, and he tilts my chin, making me look at him. "I need to know I can trust you to acknowledge your limits. You are strong—I know that. I don't want to "coddle" you. But if you won't take care of yourself, I will."

"I promise, from this point on, I will be mindful of my limitations."

"All right." He presses a sweet kiss to my lips. When he pulls back, he watches me for several long moments. "So, are we headed back to Kalae?"

I shake my head, smiling. "No. We're going to meet the others at the spring."

He raises a skeptical eyebrow.

"At a nice, unhurried pace, of course."

"Naturally."

I sit up and stretch in a deliciously lazy way. He

smiles, but his expression turns serious yet again. "You swear to me you feel good this morning?"

"Yes, I honestly do."

"All right." He sits up and runs a hand through his light brown hair, making it messier than it was moments ago. "Then I suppose we will join the others." He holds out his hand, putting his finger and thumb about an inch apart. "You realize I was this close to getting you to myself?"

"Once we finish the job, we'll spend so much time together, you'll be sick of me."

Just as I'm about to stand up, he tugs me back. "Not possible, Lady Greybrow."

I tilt my head back, relishing the sound of my new name on his lips. Then, before I can change my mind, I stand and go to help Avery prepare the horses.

It's incredible the difference a few good nights' sleep can make. I finally feel human again. My stomach is still oddly heavy, but the cramping has completely stopped. It's a weird feeling, this being pregnant bit. Terrifying at first, but strangely wonderful. I haven't admitted it to Avery yet, but I've already been pondering names. Of course, the Greybrows will probably have their own ideas about that.

What is Avery's grandmother going to say when we come back, not only married but expecting? She's going to assume the worst. Everyone is.

But that's not something I'm going to worry about now because the trail begins its ascent into the sandstone mountains. According to Sebastian's hastily-drawn map, we are nearing the spring.

Flink stays with us, close for once. Occasionally, he lifts his snout into the air as if he smells something. Whatever it is, he seems wary, which makes *me* wary.

The trail grows narrow as we pass through the rocks, and soon, it closes to a point where it will be too narrow to travel on horseback. I look up at the tall rock walls on either side of us, two canyons meeting.

"I suppose we walk," I say as I gingerly swing down from my horse.

Avery dismounts as well, but he studies the trail with narrowed eyes. "If the others are here, where are their horses?"

I crane my neck, looking about—which is ridiculous. What do I expect? They aren't going to appear out of thin air. "Do you think they already came and left?"

"Possibly," Avery says, but from the look on his face, I know he's not sure.

At the leisurely pace we took, they had to beat us here.

Unless they didn't make it at all.

"We've come this far," Avery says, holding his hand out to me.

Single file, with Avery in the front, we walk down the trail. Flink walks just ahead of us, scouting for danger.

I look up, *way* up, to the top of the cliffs, wondering

what's up there—imagining cobras raining down on our heads.

Ahead of us, the light becomes brighter, and our exit beckons. Flink hurries forward, but just as soon as he reaches the opening between the two rock walls, the dragon comes to an abrupt stop. He lowers his head, and his shoulders rise in a defensive posture.

"What's up there?" I ask Avery, but the captain's only a few feet in front of me. It's not like he can see any better than I can.

Flink inches forward, intent on whatever is in front of him. He doesn't look scared, not exactly, just hesitant. His copper scales shimmer as soon as he steps into the sunlight. Moments later, the strangest noise comes from below us.

I stop cold. "What was that?"

Avery too looks dumbfounded. "It sounded a lot like..."

There it is again, a churring noise, followed by dozens more in chorus. And it sounds just like Flink. *Lots of Flinks.*

My dragon stands there, still as stone, staring at whatever is ahead.

Pushing past Avery, I hurry forward, needing to see for myself, not able to believe what my ears are telling me.

"Oof," Avery says as his back meets the wall. "No problem. You go on ahead."

I flash him a smile over my shoulder. I didn't shove him *that* hard.

Flink's tail twitches when he hears me approach, but he doesn't bother to turn. Careful, I stay in the shadows, hopefully out of sight, and creep closer.

There, below us, bubbles a natural mineral spring. The pool is shallow, maybe a foot at most, and the water sparkles in the bright sunlight. Dark, velvety pink flowers grow on tall spikes at the water's edge.

We've found the lilies.

But my eyes only pass over the flowers because there, scattered about the edges and in the water, are dragons in many jeweled colors. And not just any dragons—lesser dragons. Dragons like Flink.

Dragons that are supposed to be all but extinct.

They watch Flink, their heads perked and their eyes eager. They continue to chirp and purr and make all the noises Flink does when he's happy or wants something.

A brave one leaves the water and inches forward. She's sleek and the color of rose quartz. Her eyes are green, as bright as a cat's, and she stares at Flink with the same adoring look he gave Queen Minerva's munchkin dragon, who he chased through the royal sitting room and onto a bookcase.

Like a chicken, Flink takes a step back. He can't go far though, and he ends up bumping right into me.

Avery whistles low behind me as soon as he spots the group. "How many are there?"

"Eleven," I say, "unless some are hiding."

The rose-colored female ambles toward us, stopping only once she notices Avery and me. She cocks her head to the side like she's never seen a human before. Possibly deciding we're soft and pale and no real threat, she continues our way. Her look is curious, a little unnerving, but it's not us she wants. It's Flink.

She chirps at him again. This time, he answers. It's a pathetic little response, barely audible, but it causes her to stretch her wings and leap back, excited.

"What element is correlated to pink?" I ask Avery, growing a bit leery.

"I haven't the slightest idea."

Flink, growing braver by the second, crawls forward. The female watches him so intently, her muscles twitch with the restraint it's taking not to run to him.

After several long minutes, Flink finally joins her. He sticks out his snout cautiously. Just when his back softens, she tackles him.

"Flink!" I yell, but Avery holds me back.

My dragon lets out an awful shriek. The female leaps away, bounding around him in a circle with unbridled glee. He pivots with her, terrified she's going to get him again. The others gather round, watching.

"She's playing," Avery says after a moment.

"Someone should tell Flink that."

He growls at the pink dragon, growing more irritated with every one of her bounces.

We watch them for several minutes, and then Avery pats my shoulder. "While Flink distracts them, I'm going to collect the lily."

I yank him back. "There are three fire dragons, one with the lightning element, and I don't want to know what the stubby little puce dragon wields. You can't just mosey on down there."

Avery turns to face me, raising an eyebrow. "I can."

Crossing my arms, I say, "And why is that?"

He leans close, looking dashing and handsome, reminding me why it was so easy to fall for him. Flashing me a cocky grin, he steps a minuscule bit closer. "Because I'm good."

I roll my eyes. "Fine. But when you come back, singed and smoking, don't expect sympathy from me."

But the dragons don't care. A few of them glance Avery's way as he walks down to the spring with the confidence of a man who belongs there, but after staring at him for a few lazy moments, they turn back to Flink, who is far more interesting.

As Avery makes his way to the lilies, my mind wanders to our group. Where are they? Surely if they'd already turned back, we would have met them on the trail.

Worry gnaws at my insides, refusing to be ignored. My mind wanders to Esme's whispered conversation with Akello.

Taking his dear sweet time, Avery browses the knee-tall flower stalks. Finally, he picks several and makes his way back to me. When he's halfway here, Flink spots him. Still half-terrified, the dragon runs to Avery like a puppy hiding behind his master.

Flink's new friend bounds after them, tail twitching like a banner in the wind. Then, without grace or stealth, she plows right into the captain, knocking him over in her attempt to get to Flink.

Avery curses at Flink as he falls, his arms pinwheeling with the lilies in his hand. He stumbles to the ground, hitting the rocky ground rump first. Suddenly more interested in the strange human than the newcomer dragon, the pink female comes closer, sniffing Avery.

"Don't move," I call to him, horrified.

What element is *pink?*

After staring at him for several minutes, she sniffs the flowers, which are still hanging in his hand. She then proceeds to eat one of the lilies, putting the whole thing in her mouth and snapping it off at the stem. Deciding Avery holds no interest to her, she steps over him as she finishes chewing.

The captain grimaces as her back taloned-foot pushes against his chest as she once again leaps after Flink. This time, Flink isn't quick enough. She has him cornered by the spring. She stretches her wings, flicks her tail behind her, and breathes a rosy fire into the air, right at my dragon.

I holler even though I know Flink's strong enough to nullify most, if not all, elemental attacks.

Momentarily dazed, he plops on his haunches and stares at her, unblinking. His eyes narrow as the enchantment fizzles, but he doesn't look as hesitant as he did a moment ago.

Relieved, I stumble against the rock wall.

Avery pulls himself to his feet, rubbing his chest with

his free hand, and climbs back up to where I wait for him.

"Charisma," he says with a groan when he gets close enough. "That's the element related to pink."

"Are you all right?" I ask as he stumbles to me.

"I thought you weren't going to ask." He flashes me a quick grin as he dusts himself off and looks back at the dragons over his shoulder. Flink now follows the female about, growing more confident.

I take the lilies from Avery. They're beautiful—exotic. The stamens glow gold in the sunlight. Hopefully, we won't need them.

Hopefully, Sebastian's already been here, Yancey's already healed, and they're on their way to Kysen Okoro as we speak.

"How are we going to get Flink?" I ask as I watch him follow his new friend about the spring. They frolic in the water and race around the edges. A few others join in, and they shimmer like living rainbows. It's a beautiful sight, but for some reason, it makes me sad.

Avery shrugs. "If we leave, perhaps he will follow."

Since neither of us is going to go down there amongst the group and snap a lead to his harness, I don't see how we have a choice.

"Whistle for him so he knows we're going," I say, and then I cover my ears.

Avery raises his knuckles to his mouth and lets out an ear-piercing whistle that echoes off the canyon walls and has every one of the dragons, including Flink, looking our way.

"Come on, Flink," I call, motioning him along. We've done this a hundred times. He knows what it means, but it's up to him to follow.

Turning, I walk back to the horses. I don't know what I'll do if he lingers. I'm too worried about the rest of our group to wrestle with the stubborn dragon at the moment. Fortunately, he appears as soon as we're on our horses.

But he's not alone.

The rose female follows him, and so do several others. I glance at Avery, unsure what to do. The captain dismounts and clips a long lead to Flink's harness, eying the others. They stay several yards away, still wary of us.

Avery steps in his stirrup, swings his leg over the saddle, and turns his horse back the way we came. Flink is reluctant to follow, but the captain doesn't give him a choice. After several moments of fussing, Flink gives in.

I glance over my shoulder, wondering how the dragons are handling the loss of their new friend.

"*Avery.*"

He turns and then narrows his eyes. Eleven lesser dragons trot along behind us, merry as can be.

"They'll grow bored and turn back soon," Avery says after several moments.

And yet several hours later, they're still there.

21

ANYTHING YOU CAN SHOOT, I CAN SHOOT BETTER

We stop at the top of a secluded ridge when twilight falls. I start a fire as Avery sets up our tent.

Once camp is prepared, we eat a small meal and tend to the horses.

Flink lies beside the crackling fire, pouting. He's on his lead because the lesser dragons are still out there, somewhere. When night fell, they went off to find a place to bed down, but I still hear their occasional calls, so I know they aren't far.

Flink wants nothing more than to go to them, but I don't want to risk losing him should they wander off before morning.

When the fire burns low, Flink tugs at his lead, belligerent.

"Stop, Flink," I say, growing irritated. He must understand: they are wild; he's a pet. He cannot go roam with them. It's not safe.

"I think I should walk him a bit before we retire," I say to Avery, scowling at my unruly beast.

Avery stands and stretches his back. "All right, but let's be quick about it."

The moon is almost full tonight, and the desert is bright enough to navigate without needing a lantern or torch. It's eerie in the pale silver light, but the silhouettes of the rocks and ridges are beautiful against the backdrop of stars. In some ways, the desert reminds me of the sea. With no forests or trees to block it, the sky stretches forever, endless.

Flink sniffs about, happy to wander. I watch for a rogue dragon to join us, but they must be asleep for the night.

Just as I'm about to tell Avery we should turn back, I spot a flickering light far out in the distance.

"That looks like a fire," I say, pointing it out to Avery.

"That's odd," he says. "We haven't seen a soul for days."

Excitement builds in my chest. "You don't think it's Sebastian, do you?"

"If it is, they aren't traveling very quickly."

"Perhaps it will take a while for Yancey to regain his strength."

Avery gives me a sideways look. "It would be dangerous to ride through the desert at this time of night and call on an unknown group."

"So you think we should?"

"Might as well." And though it's too dark to see the gleam in his eyes, I can hear it in his tone.

We head back to our own camp, which I am now glad is hidden from view, and saddle our horses. As a precaution, I slide on my bow and quiver, and Avery does the same. Leaving our belongings behind, we ride toward the fire, stopping before the group has a chance to hear us coming.

Staying low, we make our way up a hill near the camp, hoping to look down on them without being spotted. As much as I would like this to be Sebastian's group, it very well could be the men who have been sabotaging our expedition.

Perhaps it should be no surprise that it ends up being both. I suck in a quiet gasp when I spot Sebastian. He's on the ground, tied with his hands behind his back and his legs bound. Adeline's beside him, and Gorin's there as well. Yancey lies in the dirt, unmoving. I can't tell if he's dead or alive, but if he's alive, he's teetering on the edge.

Cold dread rushes through my veins, chilling me. They never made it to the spring.

Akello's near the fire, but just as I feared, the mercenary isn't on the ground. He's tossing another log on the fire, speaking low with several of his men. Esme sits in the shadows, legs pulled up to her chest, face hidden by her knees. She, however, is not restrained.

Rage replaces my initial reaction to the scene. She betrayed them. I don't know if she was working for Akello, or if Akello was working for her, but it's obvious they were in it together.

"What do we do?" I whisper low so the sound won't carry to the camp.

Avery curses under his breath as he takes in the scene. "There are five of them, excluding Esme. How good a shot are you?"

I give him a withering look, one that reminds him that I'm not known as Kalae's siren slayer for nothing.

"If I can take out three, can you handle the other two?" he asks.

"How about I handle three, and you take out two?" Then I pause. "What do you mean "take out?""

Avery shifts, looking both amused and slightly impatient. "You're not getting squeamish on me, are you? Yancey's down there, about to draw his last breath."

"I don't kill people," I hiss.

"What do you suggest then? Sprinkle them with fairy powder and hope they float away?"

Thinking, I bite the inside of my cheek. "I usually shoot just above the knee. It's not fatal, but it certainly slows them down."

"You can't make that kind of shot at this range," he argues.

I pin him with my eyes. "Excuse me? Can't make that shot?"

"You don't think they're going to sit there like ducks and wait for you to methodically take them out, do you?"

"Only one way to find out." Before my dear husband can say anything else, I draw my bow, take aim, and let the arrow fly.

I wince as the man nearest the fire screams in shock and pain—it does look like it hurts. Perhaps he shouldn't have kidnapped my friends.

The others are already looking our way and ducking for cover. They'll be after us in just a few minutes, but we have the high ground. One man, obviously drunk from the way he staggers, darts about like a dumb deer. He looks this way and that, trying to find a spot to hide. I narrow my eyes and shoot him as well.

Satisfied, I raise an eyebrow at Avery.

"It's not that difficult," he murmurs, rising to the challenge. He nocks his arrow and waits for one of them to come into view. They've slunk around the camp, and they're already crawling up the cliff, hoping to catch us. Thanks to the lovely moonlight, we see them just fine.

"Right above the knee," I say lightly. "Or it doesn't count."

Avery shoots, but instead of a leg shot, the arrow ends up embedding itself into one of the mercenary's posteriors.

"Bad shot," I say, cringing.

Avery puts his bow away. "You have no idea—I was aiming at his friend."

Two left, and one happens to be Akello. They're getting close now, too close to fight with a bow.

"Hurry—free Sebastian," Avery commands, already drawing his broadsword. "I'll take care of these two."

There's no time to argue, no time to tell him he can't fight both alone. Our best chance is freeing the others so they can assist.

Keeping low, I hurry down the ridge, skidding on loose rock in several places. Esme's already on her feet, working on Gorin's ties. Filled with fury at her betrayal, I yank her away, dagger raised.

"I'm helping you," she snarls, eying the blade.

"Just like you helped Akello ambush them?"

She yanks her arm away and goes back to her task.

"Lucia!" Sebastian demands.

He's right—there's no time to argue now. I slice through his ropes and then move to Adeline. Sebastian's already looting the mercenaries' weapons, looking for his rapier. Adeline stands, rubbing her wrists.

"Can you do any magic?" I ask. "We could use fire if you think you have it in you."

She glares at the rope burns on her delicate skin. "I think I can manage."

I turn, ready to check on Yancey, but Esme's already at his side, speaking quiet words of comfort to him and stroking his forehead. I'm not sure whether he's conscious, but his chest moves. I don't want to leave him in her care, but I don't have a choice. Avery's outnumbered.

Sebastian and Gorin race up the hill, off to join Avery. A persistent man, the one I shot first, lumbers toward them, attempting to sneak up behind the captain.

"Avery!" I yell, hoping to get his attention.

But I needn't have bothered. Adeline raises her hands, building a flame in her palms, and she heaves it through the air, right at the man. With a tremendous crash and flash of heat, the ball explodes.

I gape at the seamstress, and she smooths a wrinkle in her bodice, almost embarrassed. "I didn't know if that would work."

Sebastian attacks Akello from behind, making the man whirl around to meet him. Gorin takes out Akello's friend, and now it's three against one.

Avery ends up knocking the blade out of the mercenary's hand. It goes flying into the air, disappearing into the night.

Left with no choice, Akello surrenders.

Minutes later, Avery, Sebastian, and Gorin drag him down and toss him in front of the fire. He doesn't dare move, not with three blades pointed at his chest.

"Who hired you?" Gorin demands, furious.

Akello sags. "The prince of Guilead."

Slowly, Gorin lowers his blade. The betrayal must hurt; he looks like Akello punched him in the gut. "Daniel? *Why?*"

With a surprising amount of sympathy, Akello answers, "Why do you think?"

Gorin's expression is anguished, and he stumbles back. "He said he would support us...that he'd..."

An uncomfortable silence falls over the group.

Finally, Gorin turns to Esme. She freezes under his cold gaze. "And *you.*"

She shakes her head, her hands trembling. "You don't understand—"

"I don't want to hear it. I don't want to see you or speak with you—Esme, I don't want to *know* you."

"Gorin, please," she says, tears already running down her face. "Let me explain."

"You are my family!" he yells, overcome. "And you betrayed me! You as good as killed Yancey!"

She shakes her head, crawling to her feet. "I didn't, I swear. I mean, I did—but—"

"The crows, the cobras, the stolen mules—it was all you."

Esme looks at me, her face twisted with misery. "Not the cobras, I swear. That was Akello."

I narrow my eyes at the mercenary, but he shrugs. "They were a warning, nothing more. With your reputation, I had confidence you'd dispatch them with little difficulty—"

"Why, Esme?" Gorin demands, cutting off the mercenary.

"Akello was instructed to kill you if you reached the lily —he didn't have a choice." She begs him to understand. "I overheard him speaking to Daniel in the palace one day after a visit with Falene—I begged him to save your life. He said this was the only way. I just wanted to stop you." She looks tearfully at Yancey. "I didn't want this. Never this."

And though I don't want to, though I want to blame her and hate her and condemn her...I believe her. And I think Gorin does too. He turns his back on the group, hands clenched at his sides, and yells into the night. He's a man at the end of his tether. Desperate. Destroyed.

After several tense moments, he whirls back. "Well, job well done—you've stopped me." He tosses his hands in the air. "There is no time left to go back for the lily." He strides to her, looking her right in the eyes. "Congratulations, Esme. Aren't you proud of yourself? Don't you feel accomplished? You've killed your king."

She crosses her arms over her stomach, sobbing. "Better him than you."

He shakes his head and turns away.

"We have a lily," I say, breaking the deathly silence.

Every eye turns to me, including Akello's. The mercenary doesn't look pleased.

Avery nods. "It's true. Lucia began to feel better, and we traveled the rest of the way to the spring. We thought you'd already come and gone, but we collected a few of the flowers just in case."

Gorin stares at us blankly, as if he cannot let himself hope.

I walk over to him and take his shoulders. "Gorin, there is still time."

Sebastian steps forward. "Lucia, Avery, ride with Gorin to the king's city. You'll make it if you leave with the dawn. Adeline and I will take Yancey to the spring."

Esme looks at me so intently, I know she wants to say something.

"What is it?" I ask her.

She licks her lips and casts a fearful look at Gorin. "You said you have a few lilies, but the king only needs one." She turns to Yancey. "I could make a tea from the petals, see if I can save him." She wipes away her tears even as more come. "He's not going to hold on for another few hours, much less several days."

She's right—it's already been twelve since he was bitten. He should have passed by now. But he is strong and stubborn, and thank goodness for it.

I look at Yancey, and my heart hurts. Finally, I nod. "We have to try."

22

RIBBONS OF COLOR

With relish, Avery, Gorin, and Sebastian gather the rest of Akello's men and bind them with the very ropes that were used to hold my friends.

Avery, being the kind, giving sort, tends to the mercenaries' wounds. His current patient screams in pain as Avery removes the arrow from his leg. The captain, unconcerned, looks at him, pointing his dagger at him like an old woman would point a finger at a naughty child. "This will hurt less if you hold still."

The man curses all kinds of obscenities, and with a smile, the captain continues his work.

I return my eyes to the fire. Esme's water is just beginning to simmer. With the book Yancey found in the fortress castle at Struin Aria laid on a rock by the fire-light, open to the ancient alchemist's recipes, she counts out three of the velvet pink petals and as much glowing pollen as she can harvest. Then she adds it to the water, closes the lid, and sits back on her heels.

"Ten minutes," she says.

Sebastian nods and takes out his pocket watch.

They are the longest ten minutes known to man, and I do everything I can to keep my eyes off Yancey. I'm terrified the next time I look, his chest will be still, and he will have passed before we can save him.

The silence is punctuated with the cries of Akello's men and Avery insisting his field surgeries would go far better if the mercenaries could stop squirming.

"It's time," Sebastian says, snapping the watch closed.

With trembling hands, Esme pours the tea into a pewter cup and kneels next to our quickly-fading alchemist, being careful not to slosh the burning liquid on him.

"I need someone to open his mouth." Though she says the words quietly, she can't disguise the tremble in her voice. She's nervous this isn't going to work. We all are.

Sebastian steps forward, offering to assist. Yancey doesn't respond when Sebastian lifts his head. He's completely unconscious.

"Is he breathing?" I whisper.

Sebastian asks Adeline to fetch him a knife. She obeys without question, and Sebastian holds it in front of Yancey's nose. The metal fogs with his breath, but only barely.

"He's alive," Sebastian confirms. "But not for much longer."

The rest of us, minus Avery of course, gather round. I hold my breath as Esme takes a spoonful of the tea and drips it into Yancey's mouth.

Nothing happens.

"How much should you give him?" Adeline quietly asks.

Esme shakes her head, helpless. "I have no idea."

"Give him a bit more," Sebastian coaxes. "It can't hurt."

He might as well say Yancey's dead either way. Esme bites her lip and spoons several more doses of the lily tea into Yancey's mouth.

Suddenly, Yancey draws in a great, raspy gasp. We all go tense, waiting, hoping. But then the alchemist goes still once more. Too still.

"Yancey?" Esme says, her voice almost hysterical. "Yancey!"

Sebastian checks the man's pulse. He drops his head and shakes it. "He's gone."

"No!" Esme sobs. She rises to her feet so quickly, she spills the cup of tea. It soaks into Yancey's shirt, coating the grisly wound underneath.

I set my hand on her shoulder even as my own tears begin to flow. She collapses into me, sobs racking her tall frame. From over her shoulder, I meet Avery's gaze.

His eyes are grieved, and his expression is far more solemn than usual. He nods, understanding my pain. Esme might hold herself responsible, but she wasn't the one Yancey saved from the wretched spider. I don't feel guilty, not precisely. Just extreme, bitter sadness.

Across from me, Adeline wipes her eyes. She too wears a cloak of guilt, perhaps blaming herself for coming up with the idea to bring him in the first place. She leans against Sebastian, and he wraps her in his arms, setting his chin on her head as he draws her close.

Gorin stands nearby, grieving for many things.

And then Yancey sucks in another breath, this one stronger, louder—like a man suddenly gasping for air after nearly drowning.

We whirl to him, unbelieving, and his eyes open. He blinks at us and rubs the heels of his palms over his eyes.

"Yancey!" Esme breathes, and she flies to his side. She grasps his shoulder and sets her hand on his chest.

"What did you give me?" he croaks, sounding less than impressed as he pulls his hands down and scowls at us again.

"You're alive," Esme whispers, sounding as if she can barely believe what she sees with her own eyes.

He sits up, and she laughs even as the tears continue to stream down her face. He stares at her as if she's an apparition.

"You look as if you've seen a ghost." I kneel on his other side.

He turns to me, studying me as well. "The colors."

I glance at Avery, who's joined us. "What does he mean?"

"Colors," Yancey says, obviously frustrated. "You all

have flittin' fairy colors dancing around you like ribbons of light. What the oblivion did you do to me?"

"I made tea from the lily," Esme explains, pointing to the journal, which lays discarded in the sand. "We gave you a few spoonfuls."

He glances at her again, and then looks away as if it hurts. He then rolls up his sleeve, revealing his wounded arm.

Or not wounded.

It's healed, perfectly knitted.

"Impossible," he whispers. "Why's the fabric wet?"

"I spilled the tea," Esme admits.

His eyes widen. "The colors are changing."

"*What* colors?" Avery asks, looking at Yancey as if the alchemist didn't come back to us with his mind completely intact.

Yancey purses his lips, probably not liking the captain's tone.

"Come on," Avery says, getting a rotten look on his face. "For research purposes—what did the lily do to you?"

"Most of you are wrapped in shades of light blue and yellow," Yancey finally admits. "Esme has gold as well, but when she admitted she spilled the tea, half the ribbons turned an olive color. And now every single one of you is streaked with gray—but only since I started speaking."

I marvel at his words. "Could you be *seeing* emotion?"

"That's the most asinine thing I've ever heard." He scowls as he watches us. "Maybe."

"Sebastian," Avery says, not missing a beat, "kiss Adeline."

Adeline's eyes go wide, and just when I expect Sebastian to make a fuss, he pulls her close and presses his lips to hers. She goes limp in his arms, looking as if she's about to melt at his feet.

"What color?" Avery demands.

"Red, gold." Yancey wrinkles his nose, and then he slowly turns to Esme as if something just struck him. "*Gold*."

She flushes, unsure how to respond.

I bite my lip, trying not to laugh. "All right. We'll deal with this strange development later." I turn to Gorin. "We have a king to save, and you have a princess to marry."

23
FLOWER FOR A KING

The palace in the king's city of Kysen Okoro is nothing if not ostentatious. It stands to the south, towering over the city like a giant snowflake in the desert. It has more sleek, white spires than I can count, and it glistens in the sunshine.

"Was it dusted with mica?" I ask Gorin as we approach.

He shakes his head. "It's an enchantment."

"Who could live here?" I shade my eyes. "I already have a headache."

Gorin only laughs. He's a different person now. It's as if the weight he's been carrying has been lifted from his shoulders. It took nine days to travel to the king's city, giving us only hours to spare. Tomorrow is the first day of summer.

But we are here. And we have the lily.

People part for us as we travel through the streets. Perhaps it's because they recognize Gorin and have heard of his mission; maybe it's because our scouting group's reputation has spread throughout Elrija. I happen to think it's because we lead Akello and his men, bound and gagged, atop their horses behind us.

My heart is light. Our easiest expedition ended up being one of our most difficult, but we persevered, and we were successful.

As I ride, I set my hand on my stomach. I passed my thirteenth week yesterday, and there is no hiding the news of the baby now. Avery assures me I look lovely, but he is obligated to say so. And I don't feel lovely—I feel bloated. My trousers no longer fit, and I had to trade them for one of Adeline's dresses.

The seamstress asked me last night if I've felt the baby move yet, and now I'm constantly waiting, wondering.

Soon, we will go home. Just the thought makes me smile. I cannot wait to leave the desert behind. Flink however, might disagree. The lesser dragons followed us all this way, stopping just outside Kysen Okoro. Halfway to the king's city, I gave up on keeping Flink on the tether, and I let him travel with them. He stays close, never wandering too far, but I am worried.

I'm not sure he's going to want to leave Elrija.

"Are the colors overwhelming?" I ask Yancey, who rides just behind me. He's made a miraculous recovery, even if it's disconcerting that he now looks several years younger—a side effect from the healing water in the lily.

He shakes his head. "They faded a few days ago."

Nothing wrong with that. It was a bit disconcerting

the way he'd watch people—it was almost as if he could read your mind. The only upside is that I think he realized that we truly like him, and he's been a smidgen nicer.

"You know, you have to stop almost dying on these expeditions, or I'm not going to take you anymore," I say.

He rolls his eyes. "I doubt that. No one ever seems to ask if I want to join you."

"Oh, don't give me that. You love us, Yancey."

Shaking his head, hiding a smile, he nudges his horse ahead. Not finished, I hurry to catch up to him. "You bought the primtea for me in Malka, didn't you? When you found out I was expecting?"

His face darkens, and he looks embarrassed to admit he did something caring.

"Thank you," I say softly.

Finally, he looks at me. "I'm glad you're all right."

"And I'm glad you came with us."

I let him go, knowing this was as much of a heart-to-heart as either of us can handle. Avery takes Yancey's place, riding next to me in the streets. He waves to several little girls, not even ten years old, who stare up at him like he's a prince in a royal parade. They giggle to each other, besotted.

"How do you do that?" I demand, laughing.

The captain shrugs. "People like me."

Finally, we reach the glittering palace. Guards race forward to meet Gorin, and attendants and maids flood from the castle.

"Once again, our reputation precedes us," Avery jokes.

But it's Gorin they're cheering—one of their own, a simple man who came back to save the king from certain death and marry the princess he loves. It's a minstrel's song come to life.

Gorin speaks with the guards, motioning to Akello and his men, explaining their treason against Elrija. Wasting no time, the guards take them into custody.

Avery helps me down from my horse, and our group is escorted into the palace. I carry the lily in my pack. It's safely wrapped in a damp piece of muslin, just how Baron Malcomny instructed us to transport his beloved orchid cutting. The flower's faded a bit, but it's doing well considering the heat of the desert is scorching now.

Two guards in sleeveless leather armor escort us into the throne room, but the thrones are empty.

"Wait here," one of the guards instructs.

I unwrap the lily with great care and hand the flower to Gorin.

He catches my hand before I can step away. "Lucia—thank you."

"Of course."

"No, not just for agreeing to come with me." His dark brown eyes are earnest. "For finding me that night, for taking my charm to track down your phoenix. If it weren't for you, we wouldn't be standing here."

A little choked up, I nod.

Several official-looking types filter in, including a

young man with a stony expression. His eyes settle on Gorin, and he looks nothing less than murderous.

"Who's that?" I whisper, trying to be inconspicuous about it.

Gorin follows my eyes, and pain crosses his features. "Daniel—the prince of Guilead."

"Why is he here?" I hiss at a whisper. "He committed treason against Elrija."

"I couldn't tell the king's men he hired Akello—I had no proof."

Before I can respond, twin trumpets sound from the side of the room. Princess Falene walks out, dressed in a gown of scarlet and burnt orange. Her dark eyes search the crowd. When she finds Gorin, her cheeks flush, and she looks like it's taking every ounce of her willpower not to run to him.

He watches her, his expression just as intent.

A moment later, her father joins her. He walks with the assistance of two men, though it looks as if he is so frail he could not possibly hold his own weight. His hair is white and thin, and his face and skin are deeply wrinkled. It's obvious he's unwell.

Gorin lets out a startled noise, perhaps not expecting to see his monarch in such an advanced state of deterioration.

The king's steward comes forward, formally addressing our group. "Gorin, have you returned with the lily?"

"I have." Gorin steps forward, holding the flower in front of him, offering it to the king.

Chatter breaks out around us.

The king watches with milky eyes, but he seems alert. Eager, even. The other man at his side steps forward. "Bring it to me."

Gorin goes forward and bows. "Master Physician."

The lily is passed safely out of Gorin's hands, and I let out a relieved breath. Our part is complete.

"We found a journal as well. It belonged to the alchemist who worked with the flowers," Gorin says. "You may have it if you would like."

The physician nods, and Yancey brings it forward, flipping to the page and nodding with respect. The man reads it over, his eyes lighting with fascination.

"You have done well, Gorin."

He turns to leave, and the princess steps forward, blocking his exit. "I will join you as you make the concoction."

Her voice is strong; it doesn't waver. She's not timid or shy, and her boldness doesn't take the physician by surprise.

"Of course, Your Highness."

With one last radiant glance over her shoulder at Gorin, she leaves the throne room. We are not dismissed, so we wait for the physician's return.

"How long do you think it will take?" I murmur to Yancey.

He answers with a subtle shrug. "Making a concoction of this sort is far more difficult than brewing a simple tea to cure a spider's bite."

Thirty minutes pass, then fifteen more. The king's

eyes droop, and he falls asleep on his throne. Finally, the princess returns with a glowing vial in her hand. The physician walks behind her, elated. It must have worked.

Falene kneels in front of her father, gently waking him. She murmurs words of encouragement, and then she coaxes him to take the glowing liquid.

He winces as if the taste is bitter, but he drinks the entire vial. People crane their necks, hoping for a better look, waiting for the transformation to take place—waiting for their king to return to his youthful state.

But nothing happens, nothing at all.

Yancey shakes his head, frowning. "It should have worked by now."

"Should she have poured it over him?" I ask, remembering the effect it had on Yancey's bite.

"It's an internal disease—it doesn't work the same way."

We continue to wait in silence. The more time goes by, the more horrified the princess becomes. She blinks back tears, and her shoulders shake.

After an hour, the physician looks at the steward and shakes his head. Then he sets a hand on Falene's shoulder, offering her comfort.

"No!" she says, breaking the silence. "It was supposed to work." She looks right at the physician, livid. "You swore it would heal him!"

The man looks ashen. He takes a step back, holding his hands up in apology. "I am so deeply sorry, Your Highness."

The king clears his throat. It's a quiet noise, but all in

the room turn to face him. He looks at Gorin, his eyes anguished. With a shaking, raspy voice, he says, "You failed, Gorin. Leave—and do not come back."

Without another word, the king is escorted back to his bed, and guards usher us out of the throne room.

We failed.

But how?

We did everything right. We found the lily—we kept it alive. It healed Yancey—why didn't it work for the king?

I glance at Gorin, and then I wish I hadn't. He's destroyed. He walks numbly, his face void of expression.

THE TAVERN IS dark and smoky, and the smell of ale taints the air. It's a somber place, full of people who are nursing internal wounds and do not wish for merriment or conversation.

Our group sits at a table in the corner, nearly silent. Adeline leans against Sebastian, looking exhausted. She gives me a reassuring smile every now and then, but her eyes are too sullen to give much life to the expression. Avery sits by my side, his hand in my lap under the table, and Esme sits next to Yancey.

It cannot help that we're all paired up when Gorin just lost the love of his life. Yet even though he hasn't spoken a word since we left the palace, we're not about to leave him.

The door opens, but no one in the establishment

bothers to look over. Word of the king's imminent demise has spread throughout Kysen Okoro, and I wonder if the news is not partly responsible for the somber mood in the tavern.

A woman joins our table, taking us by surprise. Her hair is covered with a dark brown shawl, and her clothes are plain. She kneels next to Gorin.

"Falene," he gasps as soon as he sees her face.

"*Shhh.*" She glances around to see if anyone heard him. "I need to speak with you."

"I'm sorry," he says, grasping her hand. "I tried—I swear I did."

She blinks quickly. "We can't talk here. Take your friends, meet me in the gardens by the wall of climbing jasmine."

He nods, his expression saying he'd do anything for her. Somehow, he keeps his seat as she slips away. He downs his full tankard of ale in one long gulp. Avery raises his eyebrows, surprised.

"Impressive," the captain murmurs, and I elbow him lightly in the side.

"All right." Gorin smacks the tankard to the table with so much gusto, I'm surprised it doesn't shatter. "Let's go."

It feels as if we're doing something nefarious as we slink through the city, back to the palace. If any of the guards see us, we'll be tossed right back out. Fortunately, Gorin knows his way around the garden, and we find Falene without incident.

The princess rushes toward Gorin as soon as she

spots us, and she throws herself into his arms. Her shawl falls from her head, revealing her long black hair. Gorin clings to her like he'll never let go, and we all avert our eyes. The moment is painful and private, and I feel as if we're intruding on it even if we were told to come.

When they part, the princess waves to someone in the shadows. The girl takes me by surprise, and I take a step back, unsettled that I didn't notice her.

"Tell them," Falene says sternly, then she softens her voice. "Tell them so they can help."

"I've done something awful," the girl says to the ground. She's not very tall, though she's older than she looked at first glance, probably sixteen, seventeen years old.

Before the girl can continue, Avery interrupts, "Excuse me, Your Highness, but *who* is this?"

"My handmaid," Falene says, waving the question away. "Glenna, go on."

The girl wears a pinched expression, and she looks as if she truly loathes what she is about to say. "Falene's father didn't contract a rare disease."

Gorin's forehead knits, and he begins to shake his head.

"No, let her speak," Falene says before he has the chance to interrupt. Then the princess glances at us, probably wondering if we should have exchanged some sort of pleasantries, perhaps an introduction, before we got to the subject of why she's gathered us here in secret, in the darkest, most lone section of the palace garden. Then, as if deciding she doesn't care, and this is taking

217

too long as it is, she turns back to Gorin and says herself, "It's a curse, Gorin. Not a disease."

Gorin looks stunned. "Who would curse the king? And why?"

Glenna bites her lip, looking as if she's going to cry again. "I did."

Avery tenses next to me, and I do my best to hide my shock. This slip of a girl cursed Elrija's monarch? It doesn't seem possible.

"You don't understand," she continues quickly, looking ill. "Falene begged him to let her and Gorin be together; She pleaded on her knees. He wouldn't hear of it." She gulps. "Then I stumbled on this curse...and I thought I could control it. I never meant for it to go this far. It was supposed to age him a bit, play on his vanity. Make his hair gray, add a few age spots on his hands. But he started fading too quickly, and I tried to pull the magic back."

Curses deal with magic that's not at all wholesome—like that of the sirens and wraiths. They are forbidden in Kalae; only strange, bent witches in the dark forests, mad from the magic they wield, dabble in them.

"She believed the flower of the tales would work," Falene continues. "It was supposed to cure anything, anything at all."

Yancey shakes his head and looks at the princess. "Diseases are far different from curses. Your father's sickness is bound to him by magic."

Glenna turns to him. "I've tried to release the magic, but it clings to him like a barbed vine. Every time I attempt to pull it free, it digs in deeper. There must be someone who can help us. I'll admit what I've done, even if it means my death, just to save him from this end."

"You cast the spell. You're the only one who can undo it," Yancey says to Falene's maid.

The princess buries her head in her hands and lets out a strangled noise.

I step forward. "That might not be entirely true."

Yancey looks like he's about to argue with me, about to grace me with his superior magical knowledge, but Sebastian, following my mental process, beats him. "*Flink.*"

24

WHERE'S THE DRAGON WHEN YOU NEED HIM?

After following us for a week and a half, we've lost the lesser dragons. Unfortunately, we seem to have lost Flink as well.

It's early morning, two maybe three o'clock, and we've searched the desert surrounding the city for hours. There's no sign of him.

I cover a yawn with my hand.

"How are you?" Avery asks from atop his horse, right by my side.

"Exhausted." I know better than to lie to him anymore.

Avery turns his horse back toward Kysen Okoro. "We'll look more in the morning. You need sleep."

Knowing he's right, I agree without argument. I haven't seen the others for at least an hour. I think they've given up as well.

"Flink!" I call one last time, hoping wherever the

dragon is, he will hear me. I wait several moments, but he must be too far away.

Yet as we're making our way to the main trail, I hear a familiar chirp. I turn in the saddle, looking into the night. A dragon-shaped silhouette trots my way. Carefully, I drop from my horse and lower myself to my knees to greet the dragon. He rubs his head against my shoulder, happy to see me.

His feral friends are with him, but they stay several dozen yards away, watching.

"We need you tonight," I say to him.

And perhaps he understands because he doesn't put up a fuss when I attach the lead to his harness. I mount my horse and turn to the city. Without resisting, Flink walks with me.

One of the dragons, likely the rose-quartz female, calls after him, making him pause.

"Tomorrow," I promise him, and I give him a gentle tug.

The dragons don't attempt to follow us into the city, and once we near the gates, they retreat into the night.

Avery and I take Flink back to the local caravanserai, fully prepared to wake Sebastian if needed. Luck is on our side because there is no need to rouse our friends from their sleep. Our entire group stands in the courtyard, talking in hushed whispers. It looks like they just arrived as well.

When Gorin sees my dragon, he runs forward to greet us, but it doesn't look as if he has good news. "We are banned from the palace. I tried to go earlier and speak with them, tell them we might have stumbled on a different solution. They wouldn't let me enter."

"Why?" I demand. "It's not your fault the lily didn't work—the king's own physician said it was the only thing that could cure him."

Gorin huffs out a staccato sigh and gives me a help-less shrug.

I turn to Avery. "What do we do?"

He flashes me an eager smile. "We sneak in through the back. And if that doesn't work, we fight our way in. Well, except you, Lady Greybrow. I'm afraid you'll have to stay here."

"Do you honestly think I'm going to let you go without me?"

"It was worth a try."

Sebastian steps forward. "I have a compromise."

We turn to him.

"Gorin, Yancey, Esme, and I will cause a distraction—fight our way in as Avery said. Meanwhile, Falene will sneak Lucia and Adeline in with Flink."

Avery thinks about it for a moment, and then he turns to Adeline. "How confident are you in your destructive magic should you need it?"

Her lips tip with a tiny smile. "Fairly confident, Captain."·

He turns back to me and gives me a look so stern, the familial resemblance between him and Sebastian is star-tling. "Take your bow. Shoot anyone who looks at you wrong."

"Don't you think that might draw unnecessary

attention?"

"And the dragon won't?"

I smile, ready. I'm confident this will work as long as we can reach the king...and convince Flink to breathe his nullifying flames. It's not exactly something he does on command.

We sneak into the palace gardens once more, where Falene's handmaid was instructed to wait for us. She looks half-asleep, but she leaps up when she sees us.

"Tell the princess we are here and ready," Gorin instructs the girl.

She won't look him in the eye, ashamed for what she's done. Silently, she nods and then slips into the shadows, heading toward the palace.

Secure on his lead, Flink sniffs about, more than happy to be out and about in the middle of the night. Gorin paces, tense as a wild cat.

Finally, Falene appears. Gorin quickly explains our plan, as she nods, her face serious as she takes it in.

"I'll disguise them." She turns to the girl. "Glenna, hurry into my chambers. Bring two of my dresses and several scarves."

I clear my throat, mildly self-conscious, and motion to my stomach. "I'm not sure they'll fit."

Falene wears her gown cinched tight, and I'm afraid I now need something with a high waist and flowing skirt.

"Oh," the princess says, looking at me in surprise. "That's all right. Glenna, snag one of Hildi's dresses as well, but be careful about it."

"Hildi?" I ask.

SHARI L. TAPSCOTT

The princess nods, trying not to laugh. "She's my aunt. Her gowns are very...roomy."

Avery holds back a snort, and I purse my lips. All right then.

⁓

I HOLD OUT MY ARMS, horrified. Trying to be as tactful as possible, I say, "It's a bit large."

Falene scrunches her mouth to the side, studying me. "It looks like a tent on you."

Adeline, who's lovely in the Elrijan princess's marigold-yellow gown, frowns at my voluminous frock. I can tell from the look in her eyes, her mind is already working on a solution. She takes a scarf and wraps it under my bust, cinching the gown in just above my growing stomach.

The neckline dips too low, obviously intended for someone far more voluptuous than I, and the dress falls off my shoulders. Undaunted, Adeline takes another large scarf and wraps it around my shoulders, hiding the entire top half of the dress along with my bow and quiver. The fabric bulges in places, but there's nothing we can do about it.

"What do you think?" Adeline asks Falene.

The princess nods. "Better. How does it feel, Lucia?"

We've had no choice but to quickly become acquainted with the princess, what with us having to strip out of our clothing in the royal palace garden.

"I feel like a walking coat rack."

Falene grins and wraps yet another scarf around my hair, shading my face as well. "Well, as long as you *can* walk."

Flink sits on his haunches nearby, watching us quizzically. His bright amber eyes are narrowed, and I'm not sure he cares for my new outfit.

"It's all right," I assure him, holding out my hand.

He snorts, breathing out a small cloud of golden sparkles.

"Just do that again in a few minutes, and this will go perfectly," I tell him.

Glenna assists Adeline with her scarf, covering up every stray strand of her bright auburn hair. The maid's shoulders are hunched over, and she looks as if she's attempting to make herself as small as possible.

I know we're in a hurry, that we have very little time, but I can't help but ask her, "Why did you do it?"

Her eyes flicker to me, looking horrified to be addressed, and then she looks at the ground. "I wanted Falene to be happy."

The princess frowns, looking torn. It's obvious there is affection between them, but this is a rift that will take more than a night to mend.

"Do you really think the dragon can save him?" Glenna whispers.

"I know he can. *If* we can reach the royal chambers, and *if* we can make him breathe out the flame."

Then I roll my shoulders, preparing myself. Adeline hurries around the tall wall, off to tell the men we are ready.

When she comes back, Avery's at her side. His eyes widen with surprise when he takes in my ridiculous appearance. Then he grins, and my chest tightens.

This is one of the most dangerous things we've done. Avery will be going up against the king's trained guards. Someone could get hurt. Or worse.

"Please be careful," I whisper.

He gives me an incredulous look, his eyes bright. "Lucia, darling, you can either be careful or astounding —but never both."

"Then be astounding."

Kissing me softly, he says, "For you, my lady, anything—now go save a king."

I'm about to turn back to the Adeline and the princess when he grasps my hand, tugging me back. He kisses me again, just long enough I'm almost out of breath when I pull back.

"For luck," he whispers, using my words from long ago, back on the Greybrow Serpent when we were about to cross into the sirens' water for the first time.

The memory makes me long for home—but not the one I grew up in. For a ship and endless waters and mostly, Avery.

Soon.

After one last long look, Avery lets me go and walks around the wall, out of sight.

"Now we wait," the princess says.

We stand here, tensed and listening for several long minutes. Just when I begin to question whether we will hear the chaos caused by the men's distraction, we hear a loud yell.

"Come on," Falene says, and she ushers us into a small door into the palace.

I tug Flink along, trying to get him to hurry. There are new smells, and he wants to explore them all. Candles burn in iron sconces along the walls, and the dragon's scales glisten in the dancing firelight. We see no one as we hurry through the back routes of the palace, but we stay quiet anyway.

"We're almost there," Falene assures us, but as she says the words, footsteps echo from around the corner in front of us. Horrified, the princess looks at the dragon. "We must hide him!"

How?

The footsteps grow louder, and I panic and do the only thing I can think of. I straddle the dragon like he's a miniature horse and toss my huge skirt right over the top of him.

Horrified, he shifts and flails, but I hold him tight. "Flink, shhh!"

A guard turns the corner, and his eyes fall on the princess. "Your Highness, there's a situation at the gates. You should go to your chambers."

Flink twitches and wiggles, but I hold the fabric out, trying to disguise the movement. Fortunately, the man is flustered, and he never gives me or my wiggling skirt more than a passing glance.

"I will go to my father," Falene says, feigning concern.

He glances down the hall we just traveled, in a hurry. He's probably off to guard the door we just entered. "Would you like me to accompany you?"

"Of course not. I can find my way."

Bowing his head with respect, he continues at a fast clip. Once he turns the corner, I free the squirming beast.

"Honestly," I hiss at a whisper, looking Flink right in the eye. "You couldn't hold still for five seconds?"

He stares back at me, miffed.

Adeline clutches her chest. "That was the most foolish thing I've ever seen in my life. How didn't he *notice?*"

"He was preoccupied," I say as I motion for Falene to continue. "Let's hurry before we meet another."

"It's just around this corner," Falene says after we've walked another few minutes, and then she comes to an abrupt stop. "I don't know what I was thinking. There'll be guards posted outside his door—I'm sure of it."

Adeline rubs her hands together, looking nervous but determined. "I can handle them."

"How?" I demand.

"Sleeping charm."

Of course.

After taking a deep breath, she holds out her hand, silently telling us to stay, and then she turns the corner.

Sure enough, a man calls out to her, asking her to state her business.

I close my eyes, worried for her. She's come so far since we met her—grown both in strength and confidence. But she's still Adeline, and it feels like sending a kitten into the lion's den.

"I'm afraid I'm rather turned around," she says, her voice breathy and wobbling. "And I heard there is an attack at the gates?" Her voice breaks at the end, making her seem timid and overly-feminine. "Please, can you help me?"

And I realize my worrying is for naught. Immediately the men jump to her assistance, offering soothing words and bold offers of protection.

I roll my eyes. I should have expected nothing less.

"Thank you so much—I am fortunate to have stumbled into such valiant soldiers. How silly of me to get so worked up." She laughs as though she is relieved. "Feel my hands—I'm trembling."

Now surely they're not stupid enough to fall for *that*. I can't help but peek around the corner. There are two of them, both in front of her, bemused. She holds her hands out to them, and like fools, they each take one.

Instantly, a current of blue magic flows from her palms, encompassing the men. They crumple to her feet like rag dolls.

She turns to me as I step around the corner. "You know," she says, biting back a smile, "I think I'm getting better at this."

25

PRINCE OF GUILEAD

Feeling bad for the men, Adeline insists we help them into a more comfortable position—wouldn't want either of them to wake with a crick in their neck, after all.

Flink sniffs the guards, probably hoping for hidden snacks. Much to his disappointment, he finds nothing.

"Are we ready?" Falene's about to open the doors. "There might be more inside."

I hand Adeline Flink's lead. After a few awkward clothing adjustments, I pull the bow from my back and nock an arrow, but I do not draw it yet. "All right."

The princess presses the door open and enters first.

A low lamp burns in the outer chamber, but there are no more guards. Sighing with relief, Falene waves us in.

And then we see him, sitting in a chair in the shadows.

Daniel, Prince of Guilead—the man who hired Akello —stands slowly, drawing himself to his full height. It strikes me how young he looks—no older than Gorin or the princess. "Hello, Falene."

"Oh, Daniel," Falene says, sagging with relief. "We know how to save my father."

He comes to her, his face soft with sympathy, and he takes her hands in his. "Beloved, I know how hard this must be for you, especially with the loss of Gorin on top of it all, but there comes a time when we must come to terms with the inevitable."

"No, you don't understand—"

"Falene," I say quietly, my mind frantically trying to find a way to get her away from him without causing alarm.

But she ignores me completely. "The lily didn't work because it's not a disease—Father isn't sick. He's been cursed." Her face lights with excitement. "And Lucia's dragon has a nullifying element—but we must hurry. He's fading so quickly."

The prince's expression flickers at my name, and he slowly turns his eyes on Flink and then me. "Hello, Lady Adventuress. I've heard much about you." His eyes wander over the bunching fabric, and he smiles with dark humor. "Though I didn't expect you to be quite so...rotund."

His eyes drop to my bow, and he gives me a grim smile.

"We had the pleasure of meeting your good friend, Akello," I say, irked. "I'm sure he sends his regards."

"I don't suppose I have to explain to you that I'm not

going to let you or your dragon anywhere near the king, do I?"

"No, I already gathered that."

Falene looks just as surprised and confused as Gorin. This man must have played his part well.

"Forgive me," he says to the princess, and then he pulls her close, yanks a dagger from its sheath at his side, and places the blade at her throat.

"Daniel," Falene breathes, horrified.

Noise drifts from the hall just outside the room, likely more guards. What will they do when they find their princess at the edge of the prince's dagger?

"Leave now," he says, his voice eerily calm. "Take your dragon and your companions and go back to Kalae. You should have never gotten involved in our affairs."

My fingers twitch on my bow, itching to draw it. "When her father dies, Falene will become queen."

"That's rather the point, isn't it?"

"And your betrothal agreement with him will be null and void. It will be Falene's choice alone who she marries. Do you think she'll choose a man who held a blade to her throat? A man who let her father die?"

The prince's eyes flicker with indecision, and Falene stares at me, her mouth open. Apparently she never thought that far ahead. Not that I blame her—who wants to ponder the events after a parent's death?

"Let her go, and let me save him." I'm already edging toward the door leading into the king's bedchamber.

Daniel gulps. "Stop."

"You need him to live, Your Highness," I urge. "It's

the only way you'll end up with the princess—the only way you'll rule over Elrija as the prince consort."

He has no time to answer because several men rush into the room, weapons drawn. Gorin and Avery are in the lead, followed by Sebastian, Yancey, and several of the king's guards. They come to a crashing halt when they see the scene in front of them.

Gorin's face twists in a look that is nothing less than venomous, but he keeps his distance, not wanting to risk goading Daniel into doing something foolish.

"Bring me a bishop," Daniel orders the guards. When they don't move, he presses the dagger closer to Falene's neck, making her gasp. A trickle of blood runs down her skin, showing that he's serious. "*Now.*"

"Daniel," Gorin finally says, "let her go. You don't want this."

"I will marry her here, tonight. And this will be over."

His eyes have moved from me to the men, perhaps considering the female in the room to be the lesser threat —that is a deadly mistake to make. Avery sees me, and our eyes lock. He knows what I'm doing, and though he doesn't like it, he's not going to stop me.

But I need Daniel to release Falene. I don't know the prince well, but I'm afraid he is slimy enough to kill the princess the moment he feels himself losing this battle.

Too casually for the situation, Avery nudges Yancey and loudly says, "It's a sad a day when a prince feels the need to hide behind a princess."

The room goes silent.

Daniel slowly turns his eyes on my husband. "Do I know you?"

Avery leans against the door frame, lazily crossing his arms and feet. "I'm the man who bound and gagged your mercenary and brought him back to you, stretched across a horse like a sack of grain. I didn't have to cower behind a woman to do it, either."

The prince's eye twitches. "Captain Greybrow."

Avery sweeps low in a mock bow. "At your service." Then he raises an eyebrow. "Tell me, just so I'll understand, are you a novice swordsman? Do you not believe you could best Gorin in a battle of blades? I see no other reason why you'd stoop to such a cowardly level."

"I could best *you*," Daniel says, his voice low and calm.

The captain laughs in the most mocking, obnoxious way possible. It even grates on my nerves, and I know he's doing it for show. "What are you, eighteen? Perhaps nineteen years old? It's not wise to challenge a man" — Avery steps closer, drawing his sword and pointing it mockingly at the prince— "when you are still a *boy*."

Yes, that does it.

In a rage, Daniel tosses Falene aside and lunges at Avery. Before he has a chance, I let my arrow fly. It pierces the prince's shoulder and brings him to his knees.

The king's guards surround Daniel in an instant, closing in on him as he screams obscenities and curses. Avery makes his way over to me and rests his arm on my shoulders. He grins as they haul the prince from the room. "You do realize I could have taken him, don't you?"

"He called me rotund," I explain, and Avery nods as if that's a reasonable answer. "He's lucky I missed his heart."

Avery smiles knowingly. "You were ten feet away. We both know you didn't miss."

I shrug. "What can I say? I'm a forgiving person."

Gorin already has Falene in his arms. Still looking murderous, he dabs the slow trickle of blood from her throat. She turns to face me. Daniel's betrayal cloaks her like a smothering fog, and her eyes are haunted. "Please, save my father."

I look at the door, unsure for the first time. This had better work, or we're going to be in a lot of trouble.

Falene lets us into the room. The king lies atop his grand bed, mumbling in his sleep. His skin is gray and has a vaguely translucent look to it, showing the blue veins underneath.

"How are you going to convince Flink to use his element?" Avery asks quietly.

I shake my head. I have no idea.

Flink sticks his snout up in the air, sniffing the chamber. He tugs against his tether, but I hold firmly to it until I can figure out a plan.

Gorin and Falene stand near the head of the bed, anxious. Falene looks at her father. "Are you sure this won't hurt him?"

"It might be painful—I'm afraid I can't say," I answer, studying the frail king. "But it won't cause him harm."

The princess nods. "Go ahead then."

Right.

I unclip Flink's lead, still thinking of ways to coax him into using his element. When he was tiny, all it took was the slightest fright. He's not so easy to intimidate anymore.

To my great shock, once free, the dragon immediately walks over to the king, alert. He circles him several times, sniffing.

"What's he doing?" Avery asks.

I shake my head. "I haven't the slightest idea."

After several long moments, Flink stops and cocks his head, studying King Azel. The man takes a shuddering breath, exhaling a lungful of air right into Flink's face. The dragon steps back, shaking his head as if disgusted. Once he collects himself, he leans over the king, stares at him for several moments, and then—without thinking twice—breathes out a golden, sparkling flame.

Just like that.

Falene hides her face, terrified for her father. But I watch, shocked that my bumbling pet instinctively knew to use his element. After the dragon's work is finished, he flicks his tail and wanders about the room, looking for golden souvenirs.

Before our eyes, the curse falls away from the king. His skin tightens, and the color returns to his face. Hair that was thin and white thickens and turns black with a dusting of gray. The age spots fade, leaving him looking like a man of middle years should.

Falene's father blinks, understandably groggy, but his eyes are sharp and clear. His forehead knits as his gaze travels over us, but his expression softens when he finds Falene.

Overcome, the princess embraces him. "It worked."

Her father's eyes shift to Gorin. "How?"

Gorin bows, respectful, and explains who we are and why the king is alive and well. Before he can finish, Falene tells him of Daniel's treason.

He stares at us all, watching something that we cannot see.

"The colors are a side effect, Your Majesty," I say, taking a guess at what's troubling him. "They'll fade with time."

Azel nods slowly, happy to simply be alive. He thanks us profusely, and then we take our leave. The three have much to discuss. I only hope the king will keep his word and give his blessing so Falene and Gorin may marry.

News of the king's recovery spreads quickly, and soon we are mobbed with people. They congratulate and thank us, looking at us with the same reverence people tend to bestow upon siren slayers. Just another day's work, I suppose.

We find our way back to the caravanserai, where I plan to sleep for at least a week. Then we'll go back to Kalae, back home.

26
ALL THE TIME IN THE WORLD

The green cliffs of Bellaray loom in the distance. They call to me, promising respite from the desert heat, the dry, parched air, and Elrija's poisonous inhabitants. We're almost to the border village of Bale Traore. Soon, we'll be back in Kalae. I let the sheer curtain drop and rest against the soft cushions of the royal carriage.

Gorin and Falene sent us off with many thanks and an invitation to their wedding in four months' time. I'm quite sure we won't make it, but I wish them all the happiness in the world.

I set my hand on my stomach. I am fourteen weeks now, and I swear I've felt flutters. It's a strange sensation, terrifying but amazing, and suddenly it feels very real.

Prince Daniel was sent back to Guilead, disgraced. King Azel made it quite clear there would be no alliance between Elrija and the small kingdom, and if Daniel so much as sets foot in Elrija again, the prince will be executed on the spot.

Glenna, Falene's handmaid, was exiled as well, but we promised we'd find her a job in Kalae where she can start anew. As we travel, she stares out the window on the other side of the carriage. She's spoken very little, but I think she knows exile was a small punishment for her crime.

The carriage rolls to a stop once we reach Bale Traore. We'll take the Kalaen coach from here to a village in Bellaray where Gregory is supposed to meet us with Avery's carriage. From there, we'll part ways with Yancey and Esme, and then Sebastian, Adeline, Avery, and I will travel to my home village of Silverleaf to break the news of my marriage to my parents and Avery's grandmother. I'm sure it will go swimmingly.

We filter out, into the scorching sunshine one last time.

Esme wanders a few yards from the carriage and stares at the desert. I wonder if she'll miss it when she's in Kalae. Gorin forgave her for the part she played, but there is still a rift between them. After many late-night discussions, she decided to come to Kalae with us as well, or more specifically, Eromoore. She and Yancey have found something with each other, something happy, perhaps something they can build a future on.

For the first time, the alchemist smiles more than he scowls. He even laughs on occasion—though it's a terrifying sound. Still, even with Yancey by her side, it's likely difficult for Esme to leave her home kingdom.

We give her a moment to say goodbye to the desert, and I turn to the luggage rack to retrieve Flink. He's pouted since Kysen Okoro, and he stopped eating two days ago in protest.

I know he's reluctant to leave the desert, but he'll feel better once he's home—I'm sure of it.

The dragon slumps from the luggage rack and falls to his belly, kicking up a good cloud of dust.

"Come on now," I say, nudging him with my toe. "That's just pathetic."

He doesn't move. In fact, the only sign of life he gives is a loud, drawn-out sigh. Rolling my eyes, I leave him be and let him come to terms with our departure in his own mopey way.

"The coach will be here shortly," Avery says as he joins me by the fountain. He sets his arms on either side of what used to be my waist and kisses me lightly. "How are you feeling?"

"I'm ready to leave Elrija."

"I'm not sure everyone agrees." He nods toward Flink. The dragon's lying exactly where I left him, eyes staring longingly at the foothills.

As we watch, he perks his head up, listening to something in the distance. Suddenly, he jumps to his feet, more lively than he's been in days.

And then I see them, the small group of lesser dragons cresting the hill. The rose-colored female leads the group. They must have traveled day and night, just to say goodbye to Flink.

They call to him, not daring to come closer to the

small village. He turns to me, torn. He watches me for several long moments, and a lump begins to build in my throat.

"Come here, Flink," I call.

He swings his head back toward the dragons, watching them for several moments.

And that's when I realize it; he's choosing Elrija. I think I knew from the beginning he was going to, but there was that hope that he would stay with me.

Avery puts his arm around my shoulders and tugs me close. "He's a dragon, Lucia. A real dragon—not a munchkin. This might be for the best."

I blink quickly, trying to fight the sadness clawing at my chest. It's the pregnancy, that's all. I cry at everything.

But I'm fine.

Fine.

I leave Avery, needing to say goodbye to Flink by myself. Kneeling in front of the dragon, I scratch his scaly head just between his short, stubby horns, just like he likes. "It's okay," I whisper. "You can stay."

As if he knows what I'm saying, he leans against me with all his weight, just like he did when he was a baby.

The memories of tiny Flink flood back, choking me up, making me all ridiculous and watery. I hug him close, murmuring nonsense about what a good dragon he was and how much I'll miss him. And I *will* miss him—so much.

Able to tell I'm unhappy, the dragon chirps at me and butts his head against my shoulder, trying to cheer me.

"Go on then," I say, unable to prolong the inevitable any longer. I stand and wipe my eyes, then I step back, giving him space.

He looks at me, hesitant. We both know it's a final goodbye. After several long moments, he turns toward the desert, toward the dragons who adopted him as one of their own.

Avery comes up behind me and nudges me with his shoulder. "There goes three thousand denats I'll never get back."

And even as I laugh, I cry. I swipe at my eyes, feeling ridiculous. "Who cries over a dragon?" I demand.

The captain shakes his head, smiling, and pulls me close. "He'll be all right." Then he gently pushes me back, holding me at arm's length. "And you'll be as well."

I purse my lips and nod, determined to be brave.

The carriage pulls up as I watch Flink go, and our luggage is transferred.

"It's time," Sebastian says as he joins us. He lets out a resigned sigh when he spots Flink. "I thought he might."

"Oh, Lucia," Adeline almost whimpers. She too looks like she's going to burst into tears at any moment.

It's going to be a very somber ride to Eromoore.

Avery assists me into the carriage. As we pull away from Bale Traore, away from Elrija and its endless desert, I stick my head out the window, looking back.

Flink stands on the hill, surrounded by his new family, watching me go.

$\sim$

It's late by the time we reach the village in Bellaray where we plan to stay the night. Gregory should be here any day now.

Everyone's been quiet since we crossed the border, even Yancey. It's well into the early hours of the morning, and Adeline and Esme are both asleep. I've dozed on and off against Avery's shoulder, but I'm awake now. A cool breeze blows in through the window. Here, high in the mountains, it's almost cold.

The elevation rose quickly after we passed into Kalae, and the temperatures cooled. I'm going to need a cloak in the evenings until we drop into the lower provinces.

The inn is tiny in the sleepy village, but they are able to provide us with rooms. I am happy to let Avery make the arrangements. He opens the door and gallantly motions me in first. "Lady Greybrow."

I think he likes saying it as much as I like hearing it.

A fire crackles in the hearth, making the small room warm and cozy. There are quilts on the bed, a small bouquet of flowers on the nightstand, and a tea kettle on the hearth. It's as Kalaen as a room can get.

"Glad to be home?" Avery asks as he comes up behind me and rests his hands on my shoulders.

I lean my head back against his chest. "So glad."

He brushes my hair aside and softly kisses my neck, eventually moving to my shoulder. And though it's late, I sigh and enjoy the sensation. I turn into him, meeting his kiss. Slowly, the tension builds, and the heat grows.

But I pull away.

"I look like a cow," I whisper. "You can't possibly want me like this."

Scoffing, Avery picks me up and lays me on the bed. He kisses my cheeks and my throat, taking his time. "You're beautiful." Slowly, he moves to my stomach, kissing me as if I'm fragile and perfect and cherished. "And enticing." He looks up, waiting until I meet his eyes. "And there will never be a day I don't want you."

"How long will you stay with your family?" Adeline asks me as she passes the plate of bland Kalaen brown bread and freshly churned butter—both taste like heaven after our spicy Elrijan diet.

There was dew on the windows this morning, and the air is crisp and fresh. Yancey and Esme are outside now, taking a walk. She's enchanted with the forest, and Yancey is happy to show her more. When we first met, I felt sure I would pity the woman Yancey fell in love with. But I was wrong about him—he is sweet with Esme, gentle even.

"An hour, two at the most," I answer Adeline.

Avery rolls his eyes, chuckling. "Several days."

I wrinkle my nose. "Give or take."

Sebastian shakes his head and pushes his plate aside, looking as if he's about to broach a serious subject. He looks at Avery, his expression intent and scrutinizing. "Lucia says you want to join our partnership."

Avery flashes me an apprehensive look, but I shrug. I have no idea what Sebastian is up to.

"That's right," the captain says.

Nodding, Sebastian pulls a roll of parchment from the inside pocket of his traveling jacket. "I took the liberty of drawing up a contract."

Avery accepts it, looking as if he wants to laugh at the formality of it all, and I lean over, reading over his shoulder. I turn to Sebastian and narrow my eyes. "*Thane Inc.?* I thought we agreed we were going to come to a compromise on that."

"You agreed—I did not."

I roll my eyes. Honestly, I couldn't care less what we call it.

"No illegal transactions?" Avery asks, grinning as he looks up from the document. "What kind of man do you take me for? I am a well-respected sea captain—the son of an earl. I believe my name speaks for itself."

"Take it or leave it," Sebastian says, his tone snippy though there's humor in his eyes.

Avery studies him for several moments, and a slow grin spreads across his face.

"Sign at the bottom." Sebastian nods to the parchment.

"Partners?" Avery asks, incredulous. "You're sure about this?"

"Sign the paper, Avery."

Flashing me a cocky grin, Avery scrawls his name on the line. Sebastian stands, extending his hand. "Welcome to the business."

The captain clasps Sebastian's hand, and they shake. Adeline beams at me from across the table.

After the men part, I meet Sebastian's eyes. "Thank you," I mouth.

He only nods, but his eyes are warm.

Just when I'm about as happy as I think I can be, the door swings open. Yancey stands at the entrance, looking...off.

"What's wrong?" I ask him.

He frowns. "Gregory's just arrived, but there's something else. You'll have to come look."

We all hurry from the table, following him out the door. After all that happened in Elrija, I have no idea what to expect—but it certainly isn't a dopey-looking, copper-colored lesser dragon sprawled out in the luggage rack of Avery's newly arrived carriage.

I gasp. "*Flink.*"

The dragon churrs in greeting and stretches his belly toward the sun. I grasp Avery's arm, overcome.

He came back.

"Not him," Yancey grunts, and he points toward the edge of the forest. "*Her.*"

The rose-colored female watches us, unsure. She takes a step out, hesitant but eager, and gives us a chirpy greeting.

"The pair showed up right after Gregory," Yancey says, folding his arms. "Running down the road like stray hounds."

I turn to Avery. For once, I don't have the slightest idea how the captain will respond. He stares at me for several moments, looking as if he's searching for a way to let me down gently, and then he relents. "Fine—keep her."

Overjoyed, I toss my arms around his neck. "How are we going to get her home? Surely there's no room in the luggage rack for two dragons."

He shakes his head, laughing like he thinks we're fools. "I have no idea."

I'm about to suggest we hire another carriage to transport our trunks when Gregory walks around the side of the building.

I grin at the jack-of-all-trades mage, who's gifted both in the healing arts and destruction, elated to see him again. He raises his hand in greeting, his eyes crinkling with his smile, and then his mouth gapes open.

Apparently, Avery didn't mention my pregnancy in the letter he sent. I set my hand on my stomach, self-conscious.

Avery turns to his friend with amusement. "I convinced her to marry me."

"I see that," Gregory says.

He steps forward, frowning at my belly. The mage can be disconcerting at times, and I don't like him looking at me like that. He holds out a hand, letting magic drift over me, and then he nods as if his suspicions are confirmed.

"When are they due?" he asks.

I blink at him. "I'm sorry?"

Gregory raises an eyebrow, looking amused. "The babies? When are you expecting them?"

Avery chokes slightly, and Adeline stands to the side, looking so elated, I'm afraid she's going to float away.

"We're expecting *one*," I say, feeling faint.

The mage laughs. "If I were you, I'd consider buying an extra bassinet, *just in case.*"

Avery's driver calls to Gregory, and with an amused smile, the mage excuses himself.

I turn to my husband, but he's in as much shock as I am. Slowly, he grins. "Two babies, two dragons—do you know what that means?"

I shake my head, still trying to process it.

Setting his arm around my shoulder, he tugs me close. "We're going to have to buy that island after all."

There's something about the way he says it that makes me pause. Incredulous, I ask, "You already own one, don't you?"

Grinning, he turns me in his arms and brushes his lips over mine. "Maybe—just a little one I bought you as a wedding gift while we were in Teirn. But I wasn't lying —the paperwork was madness."

"You hadn't even proposed yet!"

Avery shrugs, a little too nonchalant. "What can I say —I'm the optimistic sort."

"Is there anything else I need to know about you, Captain?" I murmur against his lips.

"Probably." He gives me a wicked grin. "But why rush things? We have all the time in the world."

His words are a promise—a promise of love and family and plenty of future adventures.

"Let's go home," he whispers.

Home—what a beautiful word.

After spending several years searching, looking for my spot in the world, I've finally found it, right here with the pirate captain who stole my heart. There is nowhere else I'd rather be.

About the Author

USA Today bestselling author Shari L. Tapscott writes romantic fantasy adventure and contemporary romance. When she's not writing or reading, she enjoys gardening, making soap, and pretending she can sing. She loves white chocolate mochas, furry animals, spending time with her family, and characters who refuse to behave.

Tapscott lives in western Colorado with her husband, son, daughter, and several extremely spoiled pets.

SHARILTAPSCOTT.COM

Made in the USA
Coppell, TX
08 February 2024